MW01090048

HUGS

How A Dog's Unconditional Love Saved My Life

"A dog is the only thing on earth that loves you

more than he loves himself."

— Josh Billings

Second Edition © 2019 By Pete Klein. All rights reserved.

COPYRIGHT

Copyright © Pete Klein

All rights reserved. Published in the United States

by Amazon.com.

All right reserved. No part of this book may be

reproduced or transmitted in any form or by any means,

electronic or mechanical, including photocopying,

recording, or by storage and retrieval system without

written permission from the author.

Cover Art Source: ID 122820572 © Petansedlo |

Dreamstime.com

Edited by: Elisabeth Chretien

Cover Art by: Jessica Reed

Chapter One

"We should get a dog," Sam said out of the blue as she looked over at me with a huge smile.

I shook my head and continued to focus on the road through the pouring rain pounding against the windshield. I often struggled with driving at night in the rain, and this particular night was pitch-black. The darkness enveloped everything around the car that wasn't captured in the beams of light streaming from the front of the car.

"Ethan, did you hear what I said? We should get a dog."

"Yes honey, I heard you, but I have to

concentrate on the road. It's really bad out there," I said.

"I'm so sick of this rain. It's been like this for three days now. Enough already!" Sam took a deep breath and let it out slowly, as if gently trying to blow out her birthday candles.

We were on our way to dear friends Dave and Jenny's for dinner and board-games. The four of us always tried to get together every other week on Friday nights, and Sam and I always looked forward to spending time with them. Despite the weather, we were making good time. We were just a few miles away, and I was already savoring the thought of a glass of good red wine.

I glanced over at Sam and saw that she had

closed her eyes. She'd had a long week and could

never stay awake in the car, even on short rides.

She often took the opportunity to take a quick

nap.

I was now alone with my thoughts, staring

through the heavy rain at the road ahead. I looked

back over at Sam, who was now fast asleep, and

feelings of love and gratitude filled my heart. Sam

was a beautiful woman. She wasn't very tall at five

feet, two inches, but for me, her height was

perfect. Whenever we hugged, she would nestle

her head under my chin and rest it on my chest. I

often gently placed my cheek on top of her head. I

loved the way her soft black hair flowed over her

shoulders and down to her waist. The scent of her

hair was always different: sometimes coconut and other times mango. She had the most incredible deep-green eyes, and her smile and laugh had the power to turn any bad day into a delightful gift. Sam and I had met during our junior year of college, and have been married for the past eight years. I was a very lucky man.

I turned my attention back to the road, and my stomach clenched. There, just a few feet in front of the car, stood a deer right in the middle of the road.

I had no time to react, and we hit the deer head-on going about fifty miles per hour. The deer flipped up onto the hood of the car and slammed into the windshield, shattering it and sending glass fragments in all directions. The animal's antlers had punctured the glass, and one of them traveled through the airbag and pierced the top of my right forearm, slicing all the way though. The searing pain was overwhelming.

Before I could react, my eyes caught beams of light filtering around the animal on the hood of the car. They lit up the incredible destruction from the impact. Almost immediately, there was the sound of a horrific crash, my body was violently pushed against my seatbelt, and the world around me faded to black.

Chapter Two

I woke up to flashing lights all around me. A fireman was holding my arm and talking to me through the window of the car. "Sir, can you hear me?"

I was dizzy, and pain radiated throughout my body. "Where am I? What happened?" I whispered trying to catch my breath.

"You were in an accident, sir," the fireman said. "I need you to stay perfectly still, okay? We need to stabilize you before we get you out of the vehicle".

Then, like a flash of light in the darkness, Sam jumped into my mind. "Where is my wife?

Where is Sam?" I yelled through a fit of coughing.

"There was another person in the car with you, sir?"

"Yes, my wife Sam. Where is she?" I demanded.

Without responding, the fireman turned away and shouted, "We have another passenger not in the vehicle!"

I could only see the boots and lower legs of rescue workers running around the vehicle, but something about the angle of it all seemed off. Suddenly, my mind cleared, and I realized I was hanging upside down, suspended by my seatbelt. The windshield was gone, and my head was partially sticking out of the opening. My car was resting on its roof.

As the fireman who had spoken to me examined the vehicle and assessed my situation, I heard a shout in the distance: "We have another passenger here: white female!"

My heart began to race, and I yelled out, "That's my wife! That's Sam! Is she okay?"

"She's being helped, sir. There are lots of people here to help. Please stay calm and don't move," the fireman said in a slow, calming voice as he continued to examine my car.

Despite his words, anxiety coursed through me, fighting the pain I felt all over my body for supremacy.

Within moments, an ambulance arrived.

Two medics poked their heads into the car and asked how I was doing. I gave them a look that seemed to say, *are you kidding me?* They both gave me a reassuring smile. "We're going to get you out of here, okay? Just relax and try not to move." At least that wasn't going to be a problem; every time I moved, pain shot through my body.

Still, I couldn't stop thinking about Sam. "I want you guys to help Sam. I can wait," I said.

"We have medics already helping your wife, sir. Please just relax," one of them said.

The way he said it didn't make me feel any better. I yelled out, "Sam, are you okay?" but received no response. All I could hear was the sound of boots thumping against the asphalt and the blood pounding in my ears.

The fireman that had been examining my car informed the medics that I was free to move now. They placed a plastic collar around my neck, unclipped the seatbelt and began to gently pull me out through the broken windshield and onto the asphalt. They were clearly worried about my injuries and so careful with me that I felt like a priceless porcelain vase.

Once I was out of the car, they guided me onto a gurney, strapped me in, and began moving me to the ambulance. I looked around through the pouring rain to see if I could catch a glimpse of Sam, but with all the people scurrying around, I couldn't spot her. I yelled out again, "Sam, where are you? Are you okay?" But again, I received no response.

Overwhelming dread flooded my mind, and my brain seemed to lock up, showing me a constant stream of images of Sam lying in the ditch. She had to be okay. She just had to.

As the medics were loading me into the back of the ambulance, I spotted the truck that had hit our car. Its front driver's side badly damaged all the way back to the cab. Medics were inside the truck, but I couldn't see the passengers through the chaos.

Once inside the ambulance, I again asked about Sam and insisted that we not leave without her. One of the medics informed me that she was being placed in a second ambulance and that I would see her at the hospital. For now, they needed to attend to my own injuries.

I looked down to see my left leg, but the neck brace prohibited me from seeing that it was wrapped in a brace and that my shirt and jeans were covered in blood.

The medics placed an oxygen mask over my face and inserted an IV into the top of my left hand. Whatever they put in that IV soon had me feeling pretty good, and the ambulance began to move, its sirens howling.

Chapter Three

The trip to the hospital seemed to pass in the blink of an eye, most likely due to whatever they put in my IV. The world was blurry, and I faded in and out of consciousness. When we arrived at our destination, the medics gently pulled me out of the back of the ambulance and began wheeling me into the hospital ER. It could have been the medicine they gave me for the pain, but I was sure they had stopped in a garage-like building at the back of the hospital.

As we entered the building, several doctors and nurses quickly gathered around me and began quizzing the medics on my condition. I had a hard time following the conversation, but was able to

pick up that they suspected that I had multiple

fractures of the left leg. That explained the brace,

at least. Of course, whatever they had put in my

IV had by now numbed me to any pain. "No

worries here, Doc," I said with a smile. "My leg

feels fine."

"I'm sure it does," he said, smiling back at

me.

I was wheeled into a room in the ER, and

doctors and nurses continued to surround me like

a hive of bees. I was being hooked up to all kinds

of different machines when I heard the

emergency room's main doors slam open again

and people yelling. As the gurney passed my

room, I could see that it was Sam. I yelled out,

"Sam, are you okay? I love you!" Again, there was

no response.

The doctor hovering over me said that I

needed surgery for my injuries and that I was

going to sleep now. He gently placed his hand on

my chest and said that they were going to take

good care of me. That was the last thing I

remember before I faded off to sleep.

I blinked my eyes rapidly as I began to wake

up. I had no idea what time it was or even what

day it was. My mind was foggy, and it took me a

few minutes to orient myself. I saw that I was in a

different room now, but the machines around me

were similar to those I'd seen in the ER.

The nurse must have been alerted that I
was regaining consciousness, because she
appeared in my field of vision and leaned down
over me. Looking into my eyes, she said, "Hi,
Ethan. How are you feeling?"

My mind immediately went to Sam, and I
asked the nurse if I could see her.

In response, the nurse said, "I'm not sure of
Sam's condition, I'll let the doctor know you're
awake. He'll be in shortly to talk with you." With
that, she walked out.

As I lay there, flashes of memory began to
flood my mind and visions of what had happened
began to emerge. I remembered the rain pouring
down in buckets. I remembered the sound of the

deer hitting the car and the following crush of metal. And I remembered the darkness that followed. A strong sense of loathing washed over me, and I began to shake. Was this accident my fault? The heart-rate monitor just above my head began beeping wildly leading, and a nurse hurried in to ask if I was alright. I was in agony—not from the pain, which was being managed by strong medication, but rather from the excruciating pain of my limited recent memories.

I felt so alone and longed for the soothing voice and warm touch of my Sam. "Ma'am, please tell me where my wife Sam is. How she is doing? I have to know," I said as tears filled my eyes.

"The doctor is on his way. It should only be

a few more minutes," she said, adjusting the fluid

bag hanging on a post and hook next to my bed to

release more fluids into my IV.

A few moments later, as promised, the

doctor entered by room, passing the nurse as she

made her way out. The doctor walked over to my

bed, pulled up a chair, and sat down next to me.

"How are you feeling, Ethan?" he asked in a silky

smooth voice.

"I'm okay, but I really need to know what's

going on with Sam. I saw her arrive just after me,

and nobody is able to tell me anything. Please,

doctor, how is Sam doing?"

At that moment, a Chaplain walked into the

room and stood next to my bed. The doctor

reached over, gently placed his hand on my

forearm, and began to speak. "Ethan, we did all

we could, but Sam's injuries were too severe. Sam

passed away four hours ago while you were in

emergency surgery. I'm so sorry."

Everything seemed to shift into slow

motion. My body froze, and I was unable to move,

unable to speak. For a long moment, everything

seemed pause. Then, everything pulled out of

slow motion and began to race ahead, as though

trying to make up for the seconds I had just lost.

My heart started to race, and panic enveloped

me. My eyes shot from the Chaplain to the doctor

as I tried to read their faces. Everything I saw

there only confirmed what the doctor had said.

Sam was gone.

The pain in my heart and stomach was overwhelming, and I began to weep uncontrollably. "We're so sorry, Ethan," the Chaplain said, placing his hand on my forehead. Tears formed in his own eyes like perfectly round balls of water. They hung just on the edge of his eye before falling and running down the front of his shirt.

After a few minutes, the doctor asked if there was anything I needed. I told him that I just wanted to be left alone. Slowly, he and the nurses filed out. The last nurse adjusted something on the bag of liquid flowing into my IV before she left, and almost immediately, a feeling of calm washed over me, and I began to feel warm.

Whatever she had given me it was helping, but it couldn't overcome the sadness and loneliness that had hijacked my mind. Loss and guilt filled me as the movie of our accident played over and over again in my mind. How could this happen? What was I going to do now? All the plans we'd made over the ten years of our marriage began to melt away like a cube of ice under hot water.

I began to feel light-headed and was fighting to stay awake, but the medicine dripping into my IV was too strong, and I soon drifted off into unconsciousness once again, leaving behind the nightmare that was my new reality.

Chapter Four

When I woke up, I was in a different room

again. This time, the machines I was hooked up to

change as well. This new room had a huge

window off to the left, and the sun was just

beginning to crest the horizon. To my right was a

cloth divider that looked like an old shower

curtain and spanned the room from wall to wall.

There was a table against the wall beyond the foot

of my bed, and it was covered with flower

arrangements that made the room smell like

roses. It was quiet aside from the hum and low

beeping of the machines that had been my

constant companions during my stay.

One of the nurses walked in through the hallway door. "Good morning, Ethan. How are you feeling this morning?" she said with a smile.

"I'm thirsty," I replied through a horse, barely audible voice. "Could I please have some water?"

"Sure. I'll be right back with that," she said and left.

Something about the way the nurse responded caused thoughts of Sam to come rushing back, and I had a hard time fighting back tears. My eyes welled up, and I reached up to swipe them away with the top of my wrist.

A few moments later, the nurse returned with my water, another nurse and the doctor in tow.

"How are you this morning, Ethan?" the doctor asked as he examined the machines around me and some of the paper reports they had spit out over the past few hours. "Your numbers are good. I'm glad to see that you're on the mend," he added with a wink and a smile.

All this smiling irritated me. I guess its part of their job—reassuring the patient about his or her wellbeing—but I was not in the smiling mood, and it only served to frustrate me.

I asked about Sam again, and the doctor's face turned serious. He pulled up a chair and sat down beside me. "Ethan, she's right on the other side of that curtain." My heart almost leapt out of my chest, and I glanced over at the ugly shower

curtain separating me from Sam. "We brought you

to this room so that you could spend some private

time with her. Are you sure you're ready for this,

Ethan?"

I honestly didn't know if I was, but I had an

overwhelming urge to see my wife. I still couldn't

quite believe that she was gone, and a part of me

longed to hear her voice again, to hold her in my

arms, and to tell her that I loved her. Maybe I had

only dreamt that she'd died, and when the curtain

was pulled back, she'd look up at me with those

beautiful green eyes and give me a smile that

would rival the sun that was now streaming into

the room and splashing orange light on the ugly

shower curtain.

There was a moment of silence as the doctor watched me for a sign of how I wanted to proceed. Finally, I said, "Yes, please let me see her." My voice cracked as I attempted to hold back the rush of emotions threatening to overcome me again.

The doctor remained seated and reached back, sliding the curtain away to reveal my Sam lying peacefully in her bed just a few feet away. She was covered with a white sheet that only revealed her face, which was now lit up with soft glow from the morning sun.

I began to cry. "I love you Sam," I managed to choke out. My body began to shake, and tears flowed furiously. "I'm so sorry, honey. I miss you so much." I tried to reach out to touch her, but she was just out of reach. My hand shook as it hung in the air between us, and I stretched as far as I could to close the gap. I still couldn't, and finally, my arm fell to the side of the bed, exhausted by the effort. The pain of seeing her lying there was excruciating, and I became nauseous. A nurse came over and took my hand, comforting me as I lay there sobbing. I turned my head again to look at Sam, and warm tears streamed onto my pillow.

I wanted to believe that she was just asleep and would wake up and smile at me just as she had each day for the past ten years of our lives. As

I stared at her beautiful face, reality set in again, and fear and loneliness enveloped me.

"Please close the curtain," I said. "I can't do this anymore."

The doctor slowly slid the curtain closed, leaving the image of Sam lying there etched into my mind. I closed my eyes, hoping that this was all just a dream. In that moment, I wanted to die just so I could hold Sam again and tell her how much I loved her.

The doctor pressed some buttons on the machines connected to me, and they went to work again, filling my IV with medicine. Visions of Sam filled my mind and then slowly faded to darkness.

Chapter Five

I woke up to find my best friend, Steve, hovering over me, his face way too close to mine. "What are you doing?" I asked as I adjusted myself to a more comfortable position. Steve jumped back in surprise.

"Came to see how you're doing, bro," he said as he smiled and stepped further back. "I brought you something to make you feel better." He pointed to the chair at the foot of my bed. In typical Steve fashion, he had brought me a giant teddy bear.

Steve has a huge heart, but he doesn't have any sort of a filter. He's known for spewing inappropriate blather and manages his discomfort with humor. The gift was his way of showing love, so I smiled and said, "Thanks buddy."

Steve has been my best friend since seventh grade. My parents passed away in a plane crash that year when they were on their way to Europe for vacation, and Steve was the one who helped me through it. Steve and I are very different people, but our differences are what makes our friendship work. I am more conservative, dress in brand-name clothes, and hold a steady job in IT. I wear my hair in a boring, average style—short and well-groomed almost to the point of meticulousness—and I am always clean-shaven. Steve, on the other hand, lives a bit differently.

His clothes are always disheveled and often dirty.

He wears his hair long, well past the middle of his

back, and despite my insistence that he shave it

off, he sports a cheesy mustache that makes him

look like a seventies' porn star. He is a womanizer,

a drinker, and a pot smoker, and he hasn't held a

steady job his entire life. Steve also comes from a

very wealthy family, so having a job isn't really a

high priority for him. Despite all our differences,

he was the one who introduced me to Sam, and

when the chips are down, he's always been right

there by my side. I couldn't imagine my life

without him, and I consider him family.

Steve walked over, shoved the oversized

teddy bear off the chair, and watched it bounce a

couple of times before coming to rest on the floor

under the window. "She's a feisty one," he said

and burst out laughing.

I chuckled a little. It was the first time I had

laughed in what felt like a very long time, and it

felt good. This crazy guy could always make me

feel better, even during my darkest times.

"Where is she?" Steve asked after a few

moments. His face was now serious. I knew whom

he was referring to.

"On the other side of that curtain," I said,

pointing to where I had last seen Sam.

"Really? Can I look?" he asked, slowing

getting up from his chair.

"I guess," I said, looking down and fidgeting

with the tape on my IV.

Steve walked over to the curtain and slowly slid it open. He stood there frozen for a long moment, staring into the other side of the room. Then he pulled the curtain closed, turned to me with tears in his eyes, and said, "We got through your parents' death together. We'll get through this together, too." He walked over to me and pulled me into a bear-hug that nearly took my breath away.

The door to my room swung open, and in walked one of my nurses. She surveyed the room and, catching a glimpse of the bear on the floor, quizzically asked, "What is that doing here?"

Steve stepped out of our embrace and

smiled at the nurse innocently. "I don't know.

Ethan asked me to bring it," he said, watching her

for a reaction.

"No!" I gasped, embarrassed. "It's just my

friend's idea of cheering me up." I tossed Steve an

annoyed look.

"Well, you're a good friend, Steve," the

nurse deadpanned, playing along. She walked

over to my bedside to check on one of my

machines. "Your readings look good. How do you

feel?" she asked, placing a hand on my arm.

"Good, I guess."

"He's fine. He's just lazy," Steve said sitting

back down in the chair.

The nurse rolled her eyes. "Well, it's time

for your sponge bath, so…"

"Great! Where do you want me?" Steve exclaimed with a huge smile.

"Nice try, but you have to step out for a bit," the nurse said, pointing to the door.

"Fine," Steve said, mock-disappointed. "I'll check on you later." He slipped out into the hallway, leaving me alone with the nurse.

"He's quite the character," she observed as she prepared the water and towels for my daily bath.

"Yeah, he's something."

The next few days passed in a similar fashion. My injuries were healing, but my heart was still broken. I cried often during those days in the hospital and thought about what I would do

once I was back out in the world. Steve came by a

couple of times a day to spend time with me and

try to keep my mind off Sam. Each time he visited,

he brought another inappropriate gift. The nurses

found them—and him—very amusing, though I

didn't always. Still, he provided a welcome

distraction.

After about two weeks, the doctor cleared

me to go home, and Steve was the one who came

to pick me up and drive me. I checked out of the

hospital accompanied by a large bag of

prescription pills and Steve at the controls of my

new wheelchair. My new life was about to begin,

and I had no idea what I was going to do next.

Chapter Six

Being home again was harder than I thought it would be. Everything reminded me of Sam, and it felt like she had died all over again. It was tough getting around with my leg in a cast that went up to the middle of my thigh, and my right arm was bandaged from my wrist to just past my elbow, so I was working on one leg and one arm. Steve came over each day to help me clean, cook, and wash up, which was a huge help.

I came home on a Tuesday, and Sam's funeral was the following Saturday. Steve and a few of our friends helped Sam's parents with all the arrangements. I was dreading the funeral, and facing the family again. Sam's parents hadn't been thrilled with our marriage, they thought Sam could do better, and they didn't visit me in the hospital, but after ten years, I was used to such treatment.

The days leading up to the funeral passed slowly. I was constantly checking the clock, just to make sure it hadn't stopped working.

When Saturday finally arrived, Steve picked me up and drove me to the funeral. The church where it was held was bustling with people when we arrived. It was so crowded, it was hard to steer through the crowd in my wheelchair. Sam's parents glanced at me, but didn't come over to greet me. Steve leaned over and whispered in my ear, "Can you believe those pricks are blaming you for Sam's death?"

I turned and gave him a look of disbelief. Did they really believe that? I began to wonder if everyone was thinking that same thing.

We made our way into the viewing room where Sam's casket was set up. There was a long line of people waiting to see Sam one last time. Steve wheeled me right up to the front of the line and stopped beside the casket, turning my wheelchair sideways so that I could be closer to Sam.

As I looked down at her, my heart hurt, and I began to sob. She looked incredibly beautiful and young. I reached down into the casket, put my hand on hers, and whispered that I loved her. I

told her that I was so sorry for what had

happened and that I missed her so very much.

Only a few weeks ago, she had been full of life and

we had been happy together.

Visions of the accident began to race

through my mind, and I felt like I was having a

panic attack. Steve grabbed the handles of my

chair and moved me off to the side of the room,

so that I couldn't see Sam, but was still close by. I

was trying to catch my breath, and Steve placed a

reassuring hand on my shoulder, letting me know

that everything was going to be okay.

As people finished their viewing, they

stopped by me and murmured how sorry they

were for my loss. I wasn't sure I would make it through the day.

The church was beautiful and huge. Stained glass donned each window, and the sun's rays filtered in, casting rainbow colors on the pews in the main sanctuary. It smelled like old polished wood, a smell that would be etched into my mind for the remainder of my days.

Steve wheeled me down the seemingly endless aisle to the front of the church and took a seat in the first pew next to me. A stream of people began to fill the church, and I dropped my head in prayer. *Please God, take care of my Sam. She's the sweetest person you'll ever meet. Please keep her safe, make sure she's happy, and tell her that I love her very much*, I silently begged. Tears

dripped from my eyes to my lap as I prayed.

I wondered if life would ever be normal

again. I couldn't imagine going on without Sam.

Everything I'd had a passion for before now

seemed so trivial and pointless. Sam had made

everything around me better, brighter, and filled

with love. She was my rock, and now I was

floundering, trying to find my place in a world

devoid of love and purpose.

The funeral service was touching, but

painful. A few people spoke and told stories about

Sam, many of them breaking down as they

reminisced about how Sam had made their lives

so much better and how she had been the most

loving and giving person they had ever met. All of it was true. I tried to keep it together, but I melted deeper into despair and longing with each story.

Sam's father, Jim, was the last to speak. Jim was a towering man. At six feet, five inches, he was imposing, and I had been intimidated by him from the first time we'd met. He had short black hair and large eyes that sat in their sockets like bright blue boulders. He had a rather small nose and huge ears that made him look like a car with the doors open. As he stood at the front of the church, his speech in his hand, he hunched over and began to weep. His shoulders were shaking, and his other hand covered his face. My mother-in-law, Susan, got up, stood by his side, and leaned over to whisper words of encouragement.

After a few moments, Jim collected himself and began to speak. He talked about Sam as a little girl and told stories of her days in school and sports. He broke down often and strained to keep his composure through each heartfelt remembrance. When he had finished, he looked over at me and gave me a brief nod. It was the first sign of acknowledgement he had given me in years.

The pastor gave a wonderful sermon, and as the recessional music began to play, six men approached the casket. They carried Sam down the aisle. As soon as they had passed, Steve got up and pushed me into the aisle behind them. We made the agonizing walk through the church and

out to the all-black limo waiting outside. The

pallbearers gently placed the casket in the back of

the limo and closed the door. Steve took me to his

car, and we all lined up behind the hearse to begin

our journey to the cemetery.

The graveside service was emotional but

short, and we all took turns dropping a rose on

top of the casket.

Afterward, Steve asked me if I wanted to

stay for a while longer, but I was exhausted by

then and just wanted to go home. Steve took me

back to my apartment, and we sat in the living

room, talking about the service and crying

together. He must have realized the gravity of the

moment, because he offered words of

encouragement, rather than his usual humor to

lighten the mood. I appreciated that.

After a couple of hours, Steve left, and I

found myself truly alone for the second time in my

life. First, my parents had left me, and now Sam. I

made my way into the bedroom and pulled myself

up onto the bed. Lying there, all my thoughts

were of Sam, and I was so sad. I was exhausted,

and as I drifted off to sleep, I wondered what the

next day would bring.

Chapter Seven

I woke up at five a.m., which was typical for me, and I spent the first hour of my day just staring at the ceiling. Sleep hadn't come easily the night before despite the medication, and it felt like I had only been asleep for about an hour. I was still in the clothes I'd worn the previous day. My physical pain was beginning to resurface, so I reached over to the nightstand and took a couple of pain pills. Then I pulled myself out of bed and plopped down into my wheelchair next to the bed.

My morning routine was difficult and painful. Although the medication did a good job of dulling the pain, moving around still hurt, which made getting dressed and washing up a slow and often agonizing process.

When I was finally ready to begin my day, I rolled out into the kitchen to prepare my breakfast. Cold cereal was my go-to these last few days. I didn't have the mobility or energy to cook anything, and I worried that I might start a fire if I tried. I picked at my cereal for a while and ended up washing most of it down the sink.

Then I moved into the living room, swapped the wheelchair for the couch, and watched TV for a few hours. I took a nap and more medication, then went back to watching TV.

This routine went on for a couple of weeks.

Steve came over from time to time to visit. He

always had some new ridiculous story to tell me

about what had happened to him the day before,

which was a nice distraction. He also took me to

all my doctor's appointments, talking my ear off

on the ride to and from the hospital.

My injuries were healing nicely, and I was

able to stop using the wheelchair after my second

week home. This made it considerably more

convenient to get around and try to find some

normalcy in my day-to-day routine. Yet even as

my physical health was improving, my mental

health was getting worse. I felt alone and sad all

the time. Steve's visits were nice, but my joy from

them was short-lived, and I would plunge back

into a deep depression after he left.

Then, to make matters worse, my company laid me off. I wasn't surprised by the news, as I had missed a great deal of work, but it was one more setback at a time when additional setbacks were the last thing I needed.

Time seemed to pass so slowly that it felt like each day lasted forever. Each day, I would take a walk in the nearby park and sit on a park bench for a while, letting the sun warm my face. I would close my eyes and think of Sam and the life we'd had together. Sometimes these thoughts would ease my pain, but more often than not, they just made it worse. I was beginning to think I would never make it back to the person I was before the accident.

After about a month of this, I was making

my way home from the park one Friday afternoon

when I began thinking about the past and the

future. I had felt particularly hopeless lately.

Nothing in life seemed to matter anymore, and I

struggled to find any kind of happiness or

purpose. The idea of continuing this life seemed

too difficult, and my depression had become

overwhelming. For the first time in my life, the

thought of suicide provided me with some

comfort.

Arriving home, I dropped onto the couch

and turned on the TV. I stared blankly at the

screen for a couple of hours as my mind turned

over the notion of leaving this existence behind.

Maybe I would join Sam in another life and be

happy again.

I fell asleep at one point, and it was dark

when I woke. An intense feeling of despair

washed over me, and I limped into the kitchen for

a glass of water. Returning to the living room, I sat

down in the recliner next to the couch. I looked up

at the clock on the wall, which showed that it was

1:30 in the morning. A feeling of calm and

contentment welled up in me, and I realized I was

ready to leave this life behind. There was nothing

left for me here. My hands were shaking, even

though I felt more relaxed than I had in a very

long time.

I glanced over at the end table next to the couch, which was covered with brown bottles of medication, all topped with little white twist caps. All I could think about was my desire to stop the pain and suffering that seemed to have no end. I just couldn't live this way anymore.

I reached over and grabbed one of the full bottles of pills, and poured the entire contents into my mouth. I washed the pills down with my glass of water. This was my choice, and I believed it was the right one.

When I was finished, I reclined back in my chair, closed my eyes, and hoped that I would see Sam again soon and be able to hold her in my arms.

Chapter Eight

The next morning was a Saturday, and Steve

arrived to take me out for breakfast at my favorite

café. He knew I was a morning person, so he often

felt no qualms about showing up at my house at

six a.m. He knocked on the front door a few times,

but there was no answer. He used his key to

unlock the door and enter my apartment. He

closed the door behind him, threw his keys onto

the small wooden table on the wall by the door,

and yelled, "Honey, I'm home," as he turned the

corner into the living room.

Seeing me lying unconscious on the

recliner, he walked over, put his hand on my

shoulder, and said, "Buddy, no more sleeping. It's time for breakfast." I didn't respond. Steve tried again, shaking me a little. "C'mon, buddy, time to rise and shine."

That's when he saw the empty pill bottle lying on the floor next to my chair. His heart sank, and a sick feeling rose in his stomach. "Ethan, buddy, wake up!" he shouted, shaking me harder. I still didn't respond.

In a panic, Steve dropped to his knees and put his face right next to mine. I was barely breathing. "Oh no, no, no!" Steve shouted as he fumbled to get his phone out of his pocket.

Dialing 911, he quickly gave the dispatcher all the necessary information about my condition and address. "Please get here right away", he said before hanging up.

Still kneeling in front of me, Steve then began to shake me and yell, "Ethan, come on, buddy! Ethan wake up, please!" over and over again.

It only took a couple of minutes for the first responders to come flying into the room carrying all kinds of equipment and a gurney. There were three medics, two women and one man, and they asked Steve to step back. He complied, and they immediately went to work on me.

They quickly found a very weak pulse, moved me into a reclining position on the gurney, checked my airway for blockages and placed an oxygen mask on my face. Steve handed one of the

medics the bottle he found on the floor next to

my chair. "I think he took these". Reading the

label, the medic checked my pupils, they were

pinpoint as he expected. "Looks like an opioid

overdose", the medic announced and quickly

administered Naloxone to counter the drugs I had

taken.

"All right, let's move him," said another of

the paramedics. They strapped me to the gurney

and began to wheel me out.

Steve hurried after them. "Is he going to be

okay?" He shouted as the medics loaded me onto

the ambulance.

"He's in critical condition, sir. We have to

get him to the hospital right away," the head

medic explained. "Are you family?"

Steve paused and weighed his words. "No,

but I'm the only family he's got. Can I go with

him?"

The head medic nodded. "Sure. Jump in."

Steve climbed in, the back doors of the

ambulance slammed shut, and we all took off like

a shot, sirens howling and lights flashing.

Breakfast would have to wait.

Chapter Nine

The medics rushed me to the emergency room. When we arrived, Steve was asked to wait in the waiting area while I was taken through a set of metal doors and disappeared into the ER itself. Once in the emergency room, doctors and nurses went to work to save my life.

Later, after I was stable and out of immediate danger, one of the doctors summoned Steve into a private consultation room. "Do you know what happened?" he asked.

"The medics on the scene said he took opioids," Steve said.

"Is there anything else he may have taken

or done to himself? Did he consume any alcohol with these meds?"

"Not that I know. I found him in his chair and thought he was asleep. We were supposed to go out for breakfast," Steve said helplessly, sitting back in his chair.

"Okay, thank you. We'll keep you posted. Right now, we have your friend stabilized, but it's going to take some time before we're certain that he's out of the woods. Hang tight, all right?"

Steve nodded, and the doctor disappeared back into the depths of the emergency room.

I spent the rest of the day in emergency care. The hospital asked Steve to go home and promised to call him if my condition changed.

Steve called a friend and asked him to come

pick him up from the hospital. After picking up his

own car from my house, Steve went home and sat

down at his kitchen table. He knew I was

depressed, but hadn't realized just how hopeless I

had become. Of course, I always tried to put on a

happy face when Steve came over to visit, and I

was careful to hide any signs that I was capable,

let alone even thinking, of taking my own life.

The day dragged on for Steve. He passed

the time by playing solitaire at the kitchen table,

only interrupted by occasionally checking his

phone to make sure he hadn't missed a call from

the hospital.

Finally, just before six p.m., the hospital

called to let him know that I was doing better and would be released the next morning. As Steve lowered the phone, tears of relief streamed down his cheeks.

Something needed to change, and Steve was determined to make sure that happened. He was certain that if I came home and went back to my normal routine, this would happen again—and maybe I wouldn't survive this time. He had to save his friend. Steve took out a pen and some paper and began formulating a plan. He worked well into the night.

Once he was finished and satisfied that it would work, Steve slipped into bed, hoping that a new day would bring the changes that I needed.

Chapter Ten

I woke up in the hospital. My heart sank as I realized my suicide attempt had failed. Glancing over to the far corner of the hospital room, I saw Steve asleep in the chair and knew immediately that he had saved my life. "Hey, buddy," I said in a raspy voice.

Steve jolted awake in his chair, jumped up, and hurried over to my bed. Not-so-gently slamming a fist into my shoulder, he growled, "What the hell, dude?"

I didn't know what to say. I looked up at him for a long moment and then turned away.

Steve sighed, grabbed the chair he had

been sitting in, and dragged it over next to the

bed. He sat down, crossed his arms, and said,

"Okay, please explain this to me."

I turned back to him, looked Steve in the

eye, and said, "I just can't take the pain anymore. I

can't think of a reason to keep going. It's too

hard."

"I can't imagine what you're going through,

my friend," Steve said softly, "but suicide? Is it

really that bad?"

"The pain won't go away. Every single day is

a struggle, and I'm exhausted," I said, adjusting

myself on the bed.

Steve nodded. "Well, I have a plan for you,

buddy, and it starts today." Steve got up from his

chair and walked over to the window.

At that moment, the door opened, and one of my nurses walked in. "How are you feeling today, Ethan?" she said.

"Good," I relied slowly. "I feel good."

"All your tests came back normal, so we're sending you home today. We would like you to read this material before we can release you," she said, handing me a stack of pamphlets on suicide. "Also, we've made an appointment for you to visit with our in-house psychologist later today. Its standard procedure in cases like this," she said. She walked back out of the room, closing the door behind her.

I looked over at Steve, and he shrugged his

shoulders. "Well, start reading."

I read through all the pamphlets, though they didn't really help that much. About an hour later, I got dressed, and the nurse took me up to see the psychologist. Steve and I sat in the waiting room for what felt like hours, but it was really only about twenty minutes. Then, the psychologist appeared and invited me into another room. I glanced at Steve, but he waved me on like he was backing up a truck. I stood and followed the doctor into her office.

It was the nicest room I had ever seen. There were flowers everywhere, leather couches and chairs throughout the room, and a beautiful wooden desk against the far wall. There was a fire burning in the fireplace, and barely audible, yet soothing music filled the room. I was already relaxed, and we hadn't even started therapy yet.

The doctor motioned for me to sit in one of the leather chairs, and she sat down across from me, just a few feet away. "Good morning, Ethan. My name is Doctor Andrews, but you can call me Becky. It's nice to meet you," she said with a wide smile revealing perfectly white and straight teeth. She was young and very attractive. She was tall, with very long legs and dark brown hair that draped over her shoulders and hung down her back. She wore a dark-blue pantsuit that fit her lean body perfectly and dark-rimmed glasses that accentuated her deep-green eyes.

After a moment's pause, in which I wasn't sure what to say, she continued. "So let's talk about what happened last night," she said, opening the notepad on her lap.

"I tried to kill myself," I said simply with a straight face.

Becky looked up at me for a moment and then began writing in her notepad. "Why did you do that?" she asked without looking up.

I began to tell my story, keeping it simple and direct. "I lost my wife a few months ago, and each day is absolute agony. It just got to be too much. I've lost all hope that I can be happy again. My whole world revolved around her, and now that she's gone, I just can't see a reason to keep going. I'm sad all the time, I feel completely alone, and everything in my apartment reminds me of what I lost. Are those good enough reasons for you?" I ended sounding a bit more hostile than I intended, sitting back hard in my chair to show my contempt for the question. "I understand you are hurting, replied Becky, but I think your wife would want you to find comfort in her memory, and certainly wouldn't want you to hurt yourself" I crossed my arms in defiance and didn't say another word.

My therapy session lasted an hour, and most of it focused on just getting to know one another and banging away at my reasons for ending my life. I was uncomfortable with the conversation, but Becky's soft voice—and, if I were being honest, her stunning looks—made the hour go by quickly. At the end of my session, Becky's assistant scheduled me to return every week for the foreseeable future.

Back in the waiting room, Steve looked up at me expectantly. I managed to summon a brief smile for him. "How'd it go?" he asked as we walked out.

"I think this may really help me," I said with a smile.

"What's with all the smiling?"

"I'll tell you in the car," I said, not looking back at Steve.

On the drive back to my apartment, I told

Steve all about Becky and how her being

attractive was a distraction as well as a comfort.

She was very calming and excellent at her job.

After hearing my description of Becky, Steve

insisted on meeting her in hopes of getting a date.

I thought that would be a bad idea; he, of course,

disagreed.

I was feeling a bit better after my session

with Becky, and getting my feelings out in the

open, but I still dreaded going back to my

apartment. There were just too many memories

there. Walking back into my apartment was hard,

and a wave of embarrassment washed over me

when I looked at the chair that had nearly been

my final resting place.

Steve walked in behind me and plopped down on the very chair where he had found me. "You can't sit here anymore," he said, as though reading my thoughts. "In fact, I'm taking this chair with me when I leave."

"Go ahead. I never liked it anyway," I quipped, walking into the kitchen for a glass of water. "You want anything to drink?" I yelled from the kitchen.

"No, I'm good."

When I sat back down on the couch with my glass of water, Steve looked over at me with a surprisingly serious expression. "I have a plan for you," he said, "and you're going to follow it."

"Okay, let's hear it," I said and took a long

draw on my water.

"Nope, not right now. I have a few more details to iron out," he said. He stood up, grabbed the chair by its arms, and hoisted it over his head. "I'm serious. I'm taking this," he mumbled, making his way to the door. I smiled as I watched him struggle to open the door. "You going to be okay for a little while?" he asked, standing in the doorway with my chair hovering over his head.

"Yeah, I'll be fine. Don't worry, they only gave me a few pills this time" I said, and motioned for him to go. "Get outta here. I'll see you soon. Enjoy the chair!"

"Damned right, I will," he said, bumping the chair against each wall as he left.

I got up and went over to the window, where I watched Steve mount the recliner onto the roof of his car with rope. He looked ridiculous driving away with that huge chair on top of his car, and I laughed out loud at the sight.

Once he was gone, I turned, looked around the apartment, sighed, and walked into the kitchen. *I just have to get through today and take it from there*, I told myself. *I wonder what Steve has conjured up. Knowing him, it's probably epic.* I chuckled and started to make a peanut butter sandwich.

Chapter Eleven

The rest of the day dragged on, and I had a

hard time not thinking about what had happened

the night before. I continued to waver between

being ashamed for what I had done and angry that

it didn't work. I sat on the couch and scanned

through the channels on TV, but there was

nothing decent to watch, so I shut it off. I grabbed

a book from my bookshelf and started to read, but

I had trouble focusing in the words on the page.

About an hour later, Steve came flying

through the door, backwards. "My plan begins

now!" he announced dramatically as he turned

around, revealing a puppy in his arms and a huge

smile on his face.

"What do you have there?" I asked

dismissively. This seemed like another of Steve's

weird jokes.

"What I have here, my friend, is your new

buddy." Steve walked over to me and placed the

puppy in my lap. He was a beautiful chocolate lab.

He looked up at me with the bluest eyes I had

ever seen and gave a small whimper.

"I can't have dogs in this apartment, Steve.

You know that," I said, handing the puppy back to

him in annoyance.

"I know, which leads me to the second part

of my plan. You're moving," he said with a serious

look on his face.

"Moving? Are you kidding me? I just got out of the hospital. I'm not ready to move right now."

"No, I'm not, and yes, you are. I have the perfect place for you," Steve said.

"You do, huh? Well, that's not going to happen. I have to get my act together first. Then, maybe I'll think about moving when I'm ready," I said, getting up and walking over to the window.

"You are ready now. Let's go." Steve turned to open the front door.

"Where are we going?"

"We're going to look at your new place, that's where. Now let's get a move on," Steve said, motioning to the door.

I was annoyed, but I had nothing else do to.

Perhaps this little outing trip would do me good. I could always tell Steve no once I saw the place he was pushing on me.

Steve handed me the puppy as I walked out the door, and the three of us got into Steve's car. "So you took the chair off the roof?" I quipped.

"That baby looked good on top of this wreck."

"Shut up," he said affectionately, and off we went.

We drove for about two hours, and the puppy quickly fell asleep. I was worried it would wake up and pee all over me, but thankfully, that didn't happen. Eventually, Steve turned off the freeway and onto a remote rural road with a sign that read, "Rustic Road, no outlet." We were out in the sticks now, driving down tree-lined back roads.

A few miles down the road, Steve turned into a small opening in the trees and down a long gravel driveway lined by pine trees. At the end of the drive, the trees opened up to reveal a small log cabin nestled in a clearing just a few feet away from a beautiful, glass-calm lake. There wasn't another house to be seen anywhere.

I got out of the car and put the puppy down on the ground. I was certain he had to pee, and sure enough, he immediately squatted to relieve himself. When he was done, he put his paws on my leg and looked up at me, ask though asking me to pick him back up. I reached down and pulled him into my arms, and together, we all walked

toward the cabin.

Warm and comforting feelings welled up in

me as I looked out over the calm, glass-like lake.

The sun was beginning to set, spreading yellow

light across the surface of the water and creating

bright white sparkles within it. The water itself

looked black, and the surrounding pine trees were

mirrored on its surface.

"Let's go in and take a look at the place,"

Steve said, fumbling with the keys.

We walked up onto the covered porch that

spanned the entire front of the cabin and in

through the door. I put the puppy down so he

could get a look at the place from his eye level.

The cabin was small, but had been recently

renovated. Wood covered the entire interior.

There were old wooden beams on the ceiling, a

huge natural wood fireplace on the wall to the left

of the front door, and a small kitchen to the right.

Down a short hallway, there was a full bathroom

on the right, a bedroom on the left, and a huge

master bedroom with a full bath at the end of the

hall. The cabin had lots of windows, with plenty of

natural light streaming in and lighting up each

room. The living room's picture windows looked

out over the front porch and the lake. The place

couldn't have been more than a thousand square

feet, but the layout was simple and cozy.

"This is really nice, Steve, but I can't afford a

place like this," I said.

"Yes, you can. You already have, in fact," he said, sitting down on the living room floor and drawing the puppy into his lap.

"What are you talking about?" I sat down next to him and leaned back against the wall.

"I mean you own this place, my friend. I bought it for you last night while you were in the hospital."

"You're kidding," I said, staring at him open-mouthed.

"Nope. I realized that you need a change of scenery and thought this would be the best place for you," Steve said as he reached over and placed the puppy in my lap. "This is the best place for *both* of you."

"What about my apartment? I still have seven months on my lease."

"It's already taken care of. The movers are coming tomorrow to bring your stuff here. And you don't need to look for a job, Ethan. The life insurance from Sam's..." he paused here and then pushed on. "It'll be more than enough to cover your living expenses for years. Plus, now you don't have many expenses. Welcome home, buddy."

I looked around again in disbelief. The puppy propped himself up against my chest. I rubbed his ears absentmindedly, and his tail stared to wag with great vigor.

"You need a name for that mutt," Steve

said, getting up and walking toward the door. "Oh, I brought your bed over here last night, so you can stay here tonight. There are towels and toilet paper in the bathroom, and the fridge is filled with food."

"It's like a whole new start," I muttered.

"Which you really need, Ethan," Steve said before opening the door and walking out onto the porch. The puppy and I stood and followed him out. The three of us paused on the front porch and silently looked out over the serene view of the lake. "I couldn't be happier for you. This is a beautiful place," Steve said. He headed down the porch steps, turned, and threw me the keys. "I'm outta here. Enjoy the first night in your new home." With that, he got in his car, gunned the ignition, and pulled away.

I watched him disappear down the long gravel driveway, kicking up a cloud of dust in his wake. When Steve was gone, I sat down on the porch steps and stared out over the lake as the sun slid down below the horizon.

"Okay, puppy, you need a name," I said, looking down and locking eyes with him. I sat there deep in thought for some time, until it finally came to me. "Cooper, that's your new name." Not sure why I chose Cooper, but the name just seemed to fit.

Cooper gave me a proud look as if to say that he agreed that it was a good name. Then he snuggled up in my lap for another nap. *This is*

home, I thought as I leaned back to watch the

sunset.

Chapter Twelve

I woke up the next morning feeling refreshed. The sun was just beginning to crest the horizon, and the birds were singing their melodies of the new day. Cooper was snuggled up next to me and was still out like a light. I hated to wake him—he looked so comfortable—but it was time to start the day, so I patted him on the head. His little tail started wagging a mile a minute before his eyes even opened. I threw off the covers, and Cooper jumped out of bed and turned to look at me, as though he was waiting to see what I would do next. I put on my robe and slippers, and we made our way out to the porch so Cooper could do his business.

It was a beautiful crisp fall morning. The leaves were turning colors, creating an explosion of yellow and red that blanketed the forest and reflected off the lake. I warm feeling of contentment washed over Ethan as he took it all in.

Cooper navigated the stairs to and from the porch without difficulty, and then we went back inside, where I started to make my fancy pressed coffee. Cooper sniffed around the living room, and he was pretty excited about whatever scents he was picking up. Steve had remembered to bring food and bowels for the puppy, so I made sure to feed him and give him fresh water to start his day.

When my coffee was ready, I poured myself

a tall cup of the hot liquid, and we went back out

to the porch. There was an old wooden rocking

chair near the edge of the porch, so I sat down in

it. Cooper immediately hopped up into my lap.

The hot coffee gave off wisps of steam that slowly

drifted up into the cool morning air, and I took a

long draw. Cooper watched me drink, tilting his

head as though trying to figure out what I was

drinking and if maybe he should have a sip, too. I

smiled down at him and chuckled.

The phone in the pocket of my robe started

to buzz, and I reached in and fished it out.

"Morning, sunshine," Steve's voice blared through

the speaker as soon as I answered. "You sleep

well?"

"Dude, it's six o'clock in the morning. What could you possibly want?" I teased.

"I'm on my way over today with the movers. We'll be there around five o'clock, have dinner ready for us"

"Sounds good," I replied and hung up.

True to his word, at exactly five o'clock, Steve's car and a huge moving truck came roaring down the driveway, leaving a massive cloud of dust in their wake.

"Help me bring in these groceries," Steve said, getting out of his car.

As Steve and I carried in the groceries and began to put them away in the kitchen, the movers began unloading the truck. As I watched

them take furniture out of the back, I immediately

noticed that it wasn't my furniture. They were

unloading a large, deep-brown leather sofa and

chair, a new kitchen table, an unfamiliar coffee

table, fancy end tables, and unopened boxes of

kitchen items, including plates, cups, and

silverware.

"Wait, there must be some kind of

mistake," I said. "This isn't my stuff."

"Sure it is," Steve replied without looking

up.

"No, that's *not* my stuff," I said with more

authority.

Steve glanced up with a smile. "It is now,"

he said and went back to filling my new cupboards

with food.

"What do you mean? I didn't buy any of

that."

"I know," Steve said. "I did."

"Really, dude, this is too much," I

stammered, again shocked at my friend's

generosity. "You didn't have to do this."

"Well, you're not getting that chair back,

and your couch has seen better days, so I thought

you could use some new furniture. Besides, you

have a new place, so you need good new furniture

to fill it up," he said, smiling.

I shook my head and put my hand on

Steve's shoulder. "Thank you."

Cooper was busy showing the movers where to put everything. He would walk with them out to the truck, wait for the movers to come out with something new, and then follow them into the cabin, being careful not to get under foot. He watched them place each item where I asked them to and would then follow them back out to the truck again. He went back and forth like this until the truck was empty and the movers drove away.

Steve stuck around for a bit and helped me hang some art that previously covered the walls of my apartment. I'm a huge fan of Terry Redlin, whose work, coincidentally, is perfect for the cabin theme. Once all the art was hung, Steve slapped me on the back and said he had to take

off, but if I needed anything, I should just give him

a call. Cooper and I watched him drive off in a

cloud of dust and disappear through the trees.

When he was gone, I looked down and saw

that Cooper was peeing for what had to be the

tenth time that morning. When he was done, I

went inside to change out of my bathrobe and

into my "country" attire, complete with cowboy

hat and boots—if I was actually going to live out in

the Colorado country, I was going to fully embrace

the country life. Once I was ready, I whistled to

Cooper and told him that it was time to take a

walk.

We started out by heading down to the

lake. The cabin's previous owner had done a nice job of keeping up a walking trail all the way around it. The lake was the perfect size for a walk: not too long and not too short. My new boots needed some breaking in, but they were already starting to loosen up and were very comfortable. *I could end up spending the rest of my life in these boots*, I thought.

Cooper trotted along, his nose to the ground. He was excited to make some new discoveries. He stayed close to me and was constantly looking back to make sure I was right behind him. A couple of times, he got a bit far ahead, and then he would stop, sit down, wait for me to catch up, and then continue his investigation of the trail, his nose practically

scraping the grass.

About halfway around the lake, Cooper

stopped dead in his tracks with his tail pointed

straight up, not moving a muscle. I was impressed

that he was showing these hunting instincts at

such a young age and was very curious about

what he had found. As I walked up to him, a huge

drake mallard duck sprang up out of the reeds

along the lakeshore and headed off over the

water and into the trees.

Cooper looked up at me, his tail wagging

feverishly. I smiled and patted him on the head.

"Good boy, Coop. You found him," I said.

He trotted off, head high and sporting the

body language of knowing that he'd done a good

job.

We completed our walk around the lake

and headed back into the cabin. I poured Cooper a

bowl of food and made myself a ham sandwich.

Cooper downed his food like it was the first time

he had ever eaten, coughing up pieces in his rush

and re-eating them off the floor before diving

back into his bowl for more. I sat at the kitchen

table and ate my sandwich at a more leisurely

pace while watching Cooper inhale his breakfast.

I spent the rest of the day cleaning the

cabin and chopping some wood. Coop was close

to my heels almost the whole time. Evening came

quickly, and I made a nice warm fire in the

fireplace. The cabin smelled like sweet burning

wood, and I sat down in my new leather chair to

enjoy it. Cooper jumped up into my lap, put his

paws on my chest, and snuggled his soft little

head into the crook of my neck. It was the first of

many, many hugs he would give me at the end of

each day. We sat there staring at the fire and

enjoying the crackle of the logs and warm heat on

our bodies together. It was perfect.

We were both exhausted from all the fresh

air we'd gotten earlier and quickly drifted off into

a deep sleep.

Chapter Thirteen

The next morning, Coop and I woke up in the leather chair we'd fallen asleep in the night before. The fire had almost died out, and it was chilly in the cabin, so I threw a couple more logs on the fire, and it came back to life quickly.

Following my new morning routine, I let Coop out to do his business and made my morning coffee. With my steaming coffee in-hand, I went out to the porch to see what Cooper was up to. Scanning the area, I spotted him down by the bank of the lake, searching for wildlife.

I called him back, and he immediately obeyed. After I finished my coffee, we went inside so I could get ready for the day. Cooper was

excited to see my "country outfit." He had already

figured out that it signaled that we were about to

embark on an adventure. I prepared a thermos of

coffee, and out the door we went.

It was another beautiful morning. The sun

was just cresting the horizon, spraying light

through the many trees and over the glass-like

lake. As we had the day before, Cooper and I set

out along the path around the lake.

We hadn't walked more than twenty feet

when a small deer jumped out of the cattails near

us. Cooper took off in pursuit. I tried to call him

back, but he was too focused and determined to

catch that deer. My shouting fell on deaf ears.

They both quickly disappeared into the trees, and I took off after them. I was afraid that Coop would get into trouble or forget how to get back home.

About a hundred yards into the forest, I heard Cooper barking somewhere to my left. As I got closer, his barking got louder and more excited. When I could finally see him, his tail was straight up in the air, and he was going crazy with barking. I called for him, but he didn't respond. His eyes stared straight ahead.

As I walked over to him, I finally noticed what he was barking at: a black bear cub poking his head out of the reeds and looking right at us. Cooper finally looked away from the bear and up at me and stopped barking. The small cub let out a

surprisingly loud growl as I reached down to pick

up Cooper. I was told that where there is a cub,

there is a momma bear not too far away.

I was right. Suddenly, a huge black bear

lumbered of a row of trees about thirty yards

away and into the clearing where we stood. The

bear suddenly stopped and began sniffing the air.

At that moment, both Cooper and the cub belted

out a bark and a growl, respectively. The adult

bear's head snapped our way, and our eyes

locked. The nap on the bear's back went up, and

she crouched down into the weeds so that I could

only see the top of her head. I wasn't sure if she

was preparing to charge or was just attempting to

hide, so I turned and began to run.

Logically, I knew that I couldn't outrun a bear, and certainly not with a puppy in my arms, but it was all I could think to do in the moment. I just prayed that she wouldn't actually go after us. I looked back over my shoulder to see the momma bear charging through the reeds toward us. Cooper was barking feverishly, and I was running as fast as my legs would take us. Sweat began to bead up on my forehead and run down my face. I was in pretty good shape, and that sweat was more from fear than from the exertion.

I looked back over my shoulder again and didn't see the bear. I ran a little further and then came to a halt. I needed a break and was curious as to why the bear wasn't right on our heels; in

reality, I should have simply been grateful.

As I scanned the area, I noticed some

movement in the weeds beside me. I glanced over

and saw the momma bear staring back at me. We

had stopped right beside each other. After a brief

moment of panic on my part, she huffed, turned,

and led her cub away. She must have decided that

Cooper and I were no longer a threat.

Sweat was now pouring down my face, so I

decided to get out of the forest and back to the

safety of our "turf." Once we had passed through

the last of the trees and were back on the walking

path, I put Cooper down, and we continued our

walk around the lake. I kept looking back in the

direction of the bear; I was afraid she might

change her mind and decide to come after us.

Fortunately, I didn't see her again.

We did come across another duck that

jumped out of the reeds along the water and

watched him skim over the top of the lake. We

also saw a bright red cardinal and some mourning

doves cooing in the trees along the path before

arriving back at the cabin.

Once home, I did some work around the

place: raking up leaves, sweeping off the porch,

and finally, making lunch. After we ate, it was time

for a nap. I threw a couple more logs on the fire

and dropped down into my now-favorite leather

chair. Coop jumped up into my lap and once again

snuggled his cold, wet nose into the crook of my

neck. That hug was so calming and relaxing. The

heat of the fire began to warm us up, and we

dozed off together again.

Chapter Fourteen

The weeks and months went by, and

Cooper was getting big—very big. His puppyhood

seemed to pass in the blink of an eye, and before I

knew it, he was two years old and 120 pounds of

pure muscle. He looked imposing, and his bark

was low and intimidating. To meet him was

unnerving—until, that is, he heard his name. Then

his tail would start wagging, and he would jump in

your arms and give you a big kiss. His heart was

big enough to pump blood through his enormous

frame, with plenty of space and power left over to

shower endless affection on everyone he met. He

was a great big baby, but he could be protective

of me and those he deemed worthy of his trust.

One wouldn't want to get on his bad side, as many

wild animals could attest to... provided they were

still alive.

Each morning started out like many others

before it: we got up, Cooper went potty, I made

coffee and got dressed, and then we went for our

walk around the lake, taking in all the sights,

sounds, and smells that the crisp morning

provided. It was simultaneously invigorating and

calming, and we looked forward to it each day.

Coop and I were returning to the cabin from

our walk when Steve's car came barreling down

the driveway. As he got closer, I noticed that he

was pulling a boat. *What is he up to now?* I

wondered as his car came to a stop and Steve jumped out.

"Good morning, losers," he lovingly teased as he held up his arms, as if signaling a touchdown.

Cooper ran over to him and jumped into his arms, as he always did when Steve visited. They wrestled on the ground for a few minutes before Steve got up, brushed himself off, and said, "Well, you gonna help me with this or not?"

"What's the boat for?" I asked, not moving.

"It's for you and Coop, dude. Now help me unhook it."

"Where did you get it?"

"At the boat store, dummy. Where else

would I get a boat?" Steve said sarcastically.

As I examined it, I realized that Steve had brought me the most decked-out fishing boat I had ever seen. It was loaded with all kinds of bells and whistles: fish -finders, a depth-finder, a little troweling motor, a full audio system, and all the fishing gear one would need. It was fully loaded.

"This boat is brand new, Steve," I said, staring at the boat in disbelief.

"Yeah, I know," he said with a smile. "I'm not going to get you an old used piece of crap."

We unhooked the boat trailer from Steve's car and slowly rolled it to the lakeshore. At least now I had a use for the twenty-foot dock that extended from the shore out into the water. We unhooked the boat from the trailer, gently slid it into the water, and tied it to the dock. That done, I had a realization: "Why did we push this thing over here? Why didn't we just drive it down with the car?"

"I don't know," Steve barked. "I don't know how these things work." He handed me the boat's manual and started wrestling in the grass with Cooper again.

After a few minutes, I asked, "You hungry?"

He stopped playing with Cooper and sat up. "Sure, I could eat."

We went inside, he sat down at the kitchen table, and I started to make us some sandwiches.

"How are you guys been doing out here?"

Steve asked.

"We're doing great," I replied, looking down at Cooper, who was anxiously waiting for me to drop something that he could devour without even chewing it. "We take a long walk each morning, kick up some wildlife, and watch the sun come up. It's really nice."

"That's great, dude. I knew you'd like it out here. The fresh air is good for you," Steve said, grabbing Cooper by the head and scratching his ears.

I sat down at the table with a plate of sandwiches and two cans of soda for us. Of course, Cooper had to join us. He jumped up on a chair and scanned the table for his share of the food. I slid a sandwich over to him on a small plate, and he attacked it, wolfing it down within seconds.

Steve and I laughed and dug into our own sandwiches. "Man, he's gotten big," Steve observed.

"Yeah, and he seems to get bigger every day," I said, looking over at Coop. After a pause, I asked, "Steve, how did you get the money for that boat?"

"Mom and dad had some cash lying around, so I put it to good use," he said casually. He smiled and took another bite of his sandwich.

I just shook my head and continued eating. Cooper was looking back and forth between us, probably wondering if we were planning to share

any more of our food with him or if we were going

to be selfish and eat it all. I gave in and gave him

the last bite of my sandwich which he devoured

without missing a beat.

After we finished eating, the three of us

went out onto the porch. Steve and I sat down

with some cold beers and looked out over the

lake.

Steve took a long draw on his beer, leaned

back in his chair, and said, "It sure is beautiful out

here."

"Yeah, it never gets old. Each day brings

something new," I replied.

We lapsed into contented silence then,

drinking our beers. Cooper lay on the front edge of the deck at the top of the stairs. He looked relaxed, but was constantly scanning the area for critters.

After a while, Steve tilted his head back, emptied his can of beer, and announced that it was time for him to take off. He helped me pull the trailer up to the garage behind the cabin and secure it there. Then he said goodbye, jumped in his car, and took off down the driveway.

I always enjoyed Steve's visits and felt that he left too soon. He always brought us some kind of small present each time he visited. These gifts were never as grand as a brand-new boat, of course. The last time he'd visited, he'd brought a case of beef jerky, two cases of beer for me, and a

fifteen-pound bag of treats for Coop. I had joked

that I would be eating beef jerky until I was eighty.

Now, I grabbed a bag of that beef jerky and

a couple of cold beers and asked Coop if he would

like to take a boat ride.

He looked up at me as if to say, "I don't

know what that means, but it sounds fun!"

We walked down to the dock, and Coop

immediately jumped into the boat. I followed him

and checked over all the systems before starting it

up. Sure enough, Steve had even made sure that

the gas tank was full.

When I was growing up, my parents and

many members of our extended family had boats,

so I knew my way around one. I primed the engine

and fired it up. It started immediately and

hummed like a new engine should. I untied us

from the dock and slowly pulled away.

Cooper ran to the bow of the boat to

ensure that we were going in the proper direction.

He looked like George Washington crossing the

Delaware, and I chucked at the sight. We glided

around the outside of the lake, just inside the

reed-line, taking in the late-morning air. We

kicked up some mallard ducks, and I was worried

that Cooper would jump into the water after

them, but he stayed put, anxiously stomping his

front feet as if he were marching in a band.

Our first boat ride was uneventful and

soothing. As soon as we arrived back at the dock, Cooper jumped out onto the dock while we were still a few feet away. I nudged the wood and tied off the boat.

I spent the remainder of the day doing chores around the cabin: I split some more wood for the fireplace, fixed the porch railing, and playing in the leaves in the backyard with Cooper. He kept trying to pull me out, but got distracted by nearby birds and took off to chase them.

Following another long day, we retired to our favorite spot in the living room. I stoked the fire in the fireplace, and we sat in our chair together. Even though he was over a hundred pounds now, Coop still jumped up into my lap and snuggled his head into the crook of my neck, just like he had when he was a puppy. I had come to love that hug at the end of the day. I even started to rely on it.

We dozed in the chair for a few hours and then got up and headed to bed. By then, the fire was only embers giving off a soft orange glow that provided just enough light to help us make our way to the bedroom. I slid under the covers, and Cooper found his place at the foot of the bed.

Another great day was behind us, and I drifted off to sleep wondering what adventures the next would bring.

Chapter Fifteen

It was Cooper's fifth birthday, and I had big plans for us. We started the day with my traditional cupcakes—of which Cooper got one. It was only one of the very many times that Coop got "people food." I put a candle in it, sang "happy Birthday" to him, and blew it out for him. Then I peeled off the wrapper and offered it to him. He scarfed it down like it was the last food on earth, leaving some frosting on his muzzle. It made him look like a dork.

I planned to take him fishing, which was one of Cooper's favorite activities. Of course, I enjoyed it, too. I got dressed in my usual outfit. By now, I had become very comfortable in my cowboy hat and boots. Putting them on had become second nature to me, and they were worn-in and quite comfortable. I completed the outfit with an old pair of jeans, a t-shirt, and a flannel shirt over the top, which I left untucked. The mornings were usually pretty cool, but by late morning, it would warm up enough for me to shed the flannel. I filled my thermos with coffee, and away we went.

Cooper ran across the porch, down the front steps, and over to the dock. With one quick leap, he was sitting in the boat and looking back at me as if to say, "What's taking so long? Let's get this party started!"

I asked him if he was ready to catch some

fish, and he immediately became excited. He

started to pace around the boat until he finally

settled at the bow, assuming his George

Washington pose. I stepped into the boat, fired up

the engine, untied us from the dock, and guided

us out into the water.

Coop and I had a favorite spot on the lake.

It was about halfway across the lake and near a

clump of tall, thick reeds. My depth-finder

indicated that it was the deepest part of the lake,

and the fish seemed to like it there, because we

always had good luck catching all kinds of fish.

This lake had it all: walleyes, pike, bass, and plenty

of crappies. We already had a freezer full of them

back at the cabin, so I intended to throw back

anything I caught this morning, unless it was a

walleye. I just couldn't pass those up; they're by

far my favorite fish.

As we reached our favorite fishing spot, I

slowed the boat to a crawl, shut down the engine,

and tossed out the anchor. Cooper was already

looking over the side of the boat and scanning the

water for fish as I prepared the fishing rods. Once

I was all set, I threw a couple of lines into the

water and took a long draw of my hot coffee.

It wasn't long before we had a nice bite. I

set the hook and started to reel in what felt like a

good-sized catch. Coop jumped over to sit right

next to me, anxiously awaiting the prize I would

pull out of the water. He was so big that whenever he moved around in the boat, it would tilt and rock, throwing me off-balance.

Once I had reeled the fish up close to the boat, I reached for the net and scooped it up. Bingo! It was a nice-sized walleye, the perfect start to the day.

Pulling a fish into the boat was always a pure joy and an adventure. Cooper would stand completely still, staring at the fish as I removed it from the hook. Then, I would drop the fish on the floor of the boat, and that meant it was playtime! Cooper would grab the fish with his mouth and thrash it around like it was his favorite toy. Of course, the fish would often fly out of his mouth and land in random places around the boat, so Coop would chase it down and start the game all over again. This would go on until he lost interest in that particular fish and would come back over by me. He would then relax by my side until the next fish appeared.

Often, he would accidentally thrash and toss the fish overboard, look down into the water to see where it went, and then look back at me as if it was my fault. At such moments, I would just shrug and toss another line into the water.

Coop always knew when I planned to keep a particular catch, because I would take it off the hook and put it in the live-well. He would look at me as if he understood that that one was for dad.

We would fish for a few hours and then head back to the cabin. I always tried to catch one last fish before heading back, so Cooper could play with it on the ride home. If he didn't toss the fish overboard during the ride—which he often did—Cooper would jump out of the boat and onto the dock, walk to the end, and then drop the fish back in the water. Of course, the fish was always dead by then, and we'd sit together and watch it float away. I think Cooper thought he was setting it free and was just grateful for the playtime with his little buddy. I really got a kick out of that.

I tried to go fishing at least four or five times a week. We were never short on fish to eat, and it made me feel good that we were trying to live off the land. It made me appreciate the food—and nature in general—more. Both Cooper and I had changed a lot while living out in the sticks, and in my heart, I knew I wouldn't want to live any other way. My life before was filled with stress, busy days, long hours at work, and far too much fast food.

Back at the cabin, we had another cupcake and some lunch. We took a little nap in our chair for a couple of hours and then got moving again. I wanted to change things up a bit, so for our daily walk, we set off to the left of the lake through the woods. We really hadn't explored that area much, and I thought Cooper would enjoy some new territory with all its new smells.

As I had expected, Cooper was really excited and would stop every few feet to let his nose take in all the different odors. Each tree and shrub offered an opportunity not only to discover what else had been there, but also to let the world know that Cooper had been there. I was always amazed at how much pee he could splash. It seemed like he had an endless supply. Plus, being a man, I couldn't understand how he could just pee a little bit and then hold back the rest for the next tree or shrub. Once guys start, it's nearly impossible to stop the flow, but Cooper had it down to a science. He was not going to waste one drop. He had territory to claim.

Much like on all our walks, we saw birds

and rabbits. We startled a few deer and watched

them scamper off deeper into the woods. By now,

Cooper had learned that chasing deer was a waste

of effort, and he would just stand next to me and

watch them bound away, his ears perked up and

his nose in the air. We came across a small green

frog with shiny skin and little red feet. I thought

Cooper would surely pick it up in his mouth and

kill the little dude, but he didn't. He just put his

nose down on the frog's tiny back and sniffed it.

Then he tilted his head up at me with a "What the

hell is this thing?" expression. Coop then moved

on, leaving the poor frog unscathed aside from

the heart attack I was certain our new green

friend was experiencing.

After we'd walked a little further, I decided

that we'd gone far enough for the day. I whistled

to Cooper to come so we could start our walk

back to the cabin. I couldn't see him, as he had

run ahead of me, but I couldn't hear him, either,

and that worried me. I walked along a bit further

so see what was keeping him.

I entered a small clearing, and about twenty

yards away, Coop was in full point mode, not

moving a muscle, his tail straight in the air. I

hustled over to see what he had found, and it

happened just as I arrived.

Cooper jumped back suddenly and began to

shake his head and rub his face in the grass. It

took me a few seconds to realize what Cooper had

encountered: a skunk! Within moments, the odor

was overwhelming, and I began coughing and

wheezing. I felt nauseous and almost puked.

Gagging, I walked over to Cooper, who was still

rubbing his face in the grass, and kneeled down to

inspect him. His eyes were watering, and he

reeked. His whole face had been hit, and the poor

guy was having a hard time shaking it off.

Once Cooper was over the initial shock of

being sprayed, we composed ourselves and

started to walk back to the cabin.

As soon as we got home, I set to work

cleaning us up. I took Coop to the backyard, told

him to sit, and grabbed some tomato juice from

the kitchen and the hose from the garage. Tomato

juice is a classic home remedy for washing off

skunk spray, and it actually works really well. I

covered Coop in tomato juice, rubbed it in, and

then sprayed him off. I performed this exercise

four times before the smell finally subsided. Once

I was done, Coop took off across the lawn,

dropped down in the grass, and began to roll

around. While he was recovering from his bath, I

shed my clothes and left them hanging outside to

air out. Then I entered the cabin and took a long,

hot shower.

When I came out of the bathroom in my

favorite robe, I saw that Cooper had let himself in

through the doggie door and waiting for me in the

kitchen. I walked over to inspect him and, satisfied

that the smell was gone, prepared some dinner for us.

We finished our meal, then made our way into the living room to enjoy a fire in the fireplace and some time in our favorite chair. As always, Cooper jumped up into my lap and gave me that warm, wonderful Cooper hug. Both of us were exhausted from the day's adventures, and Cooper quickly dozed off. Just before I fell asleep, I thought about how grateful I was to have Cooper in my life and how happy I was living in this beautiful place.

"It doesn't get much better than this," I whispered. I chuckled a little as I thought back on our skunk encounter earlier in the day, then closed my eyes and fell asleep.

Chapter Sixteen

The next day started with a bang. Literally.

It was time to go hunting, which was another of

Cooper's favorite pastimes.

As I started to get dressed in my hunting

clothes, Cooper came over to smell what I was

putting on. His tail immediately started wagging,

and he began whining and pacing the floor with

excitement, never taking his eyes off of me. I

collected all my equipment, including a thermos

filled with hot coffee, and we headed out.

We usually took the boat out on the water

to hunt, but today, I decided to walk around the

lake and see what we could kick up instead. Over

the past couple of weeks, we had flushed out a

few pheasants, so I thought we might get lucky

and find one again today. Cooper had already

bounded ahead to the boat and was eagerly

awaiting my arrival. When I began to walk down

the trail around the lake instead of climbing into

the boat, and he looked at me and tilted his head

in confusion.

"C'mon, Coop, time to find a bird," I called

back to him.

He immediately jumped out of the boat and

into the water and swam over to me. Walking out

of the lake, he shook himself off, spraying water in

all directions, before taking his place by my side.

For some reason, he always insisted on walking on

my left side. I was never sure why; I hadn't trained

him to do that. Maybe it was because that was the

side closest to the lake.

Almost immediately, we kicked up a nice

mallard duck. It darted out of the reeds and away

from us over the water. I turned, aimed, and shot.

The duck tumbled in the air and splashed down in

the water no more than twenty yards away.

Cooper leapt into the lake in hot pursuit. He swam

out, grabbed the duck in his mouth, and swam

back to shore. Once on land, he walked over to

me and dropped the duck at my feet, just like he

had done a hundred times. He shook himself off

and looked up at me in anticipation. I reached

down, grabbed the duck, and put it in the back

pouch of my hunting jacket. Then we started

walking again.

During a normal walk, Cooper would get out

in front of me, his nose to the ground. But when

we were hunting, he stayed right by my side,

constantly looking up at me so that he was ready

to go if I shouldered my shotgun.

As we walked, we enjoyed the crisp

morning air and nature's morning songs. A slight

breeze traveled through the trees, making the

leaves flutter. The sun was just breaking over the

horizon, and it was the coldest part of the day.

Frost began to form on everything, transforming

the nighttime dew into crystals of white. Almost in

an instant, everything looked like it was covered in

snow. It was beautiful. This only lasted for a few minutes, and then the heat of the sun started to melt the crystals back into dew. It dripped from the leaves and sounded like gentle rain. Just being outside to watch nature usher in a new day was my favorite part of hunting. Cooper, on the other hand, wanted action, and it didn't take long to fulfill that desire.

Roughly fifteen yards in front of us, a huge rooster pheasant leapt out of the deep weeds, rising up like a helicopter in front of us. Pheasants are beautiful birds, covered in brown, black, red, and green, with a white circle around their necks. The only thing better than how they look is how they taste. I leveled my gun and took aim. The

HUGS

report of the gun echoed through the trees as the

pheasant cartwheeled in the air and thumped to

the ground.

Cooper was off like a shot, never taking his

eyes off the bird. That nose of his was incredible,

and it only took him a few seconds to find the

downed pheasant in the deep, thick weeds.

Trotting back to me with his prize in his mouth,

Cooper dropped it at my feet and sat down next

to me, glowing with satisfaction. I pocketed the

pheasant, and we started walking again.

During the remainder of our hunt, we

spooked a deer and watched him run off, his

white tail flickering as he bounded through the

trees. We saw cardinals and blue jays in the trees,

calling and bouncing from branch to branch.

As we neared our cabin on the other side of the lake, another duck jumped out of the reeds along the water. I took aim and fired, but missed, and we watched the duck fly off into the distance. Cooper looked up at me in disappointment. "Sorry, Coop," I said, "we can't get 'em all." I patted him on the head, and we walked up to the cabin.

Once on the porch, I took off my boots and wiped off Cooper's feet before we went in. It was late morning by now and was starting to get much warmer. "It's going to be another perfect fall day," I said to Coop as we walked into the cabin.

We had a nice big lunch and then retired to

our chair for a short nap. We snuggled up

together and dozed off, dreaming about our

hunting adventure and basking in gratitude for

our friendship.

Chapter Seventeen

Cooper and I woke up from our afternoon nap refreshed and ready to go, so I decided to do some fishing. But first, we had to clean and prepare our birds from the morning's hunt. I threw on my boots and cowboy hat, and we ventured out to the backyard, where I had built a small cleaning shack for preparing birds, fish, deer, and the occasional turkey. Cooper was always eager to help, mostly because he wanted to taste the food.

I prepared the duck and the pheasant, placed the tenderloin fillets in zip-lock bags, and took them to the kitchen. There, I pulled out a white ceramic bowl and placed the fillets in some

of my favorite marinade for dinner later. I placed

our dinner in the fridge and then started to get

ready to go fishing.

As soon as I donned my lucky fishing vest,

Cooper bounded out the door, across the front

lawn, and into the boat. He then turned and sat

down to wait for me to arrive.

I joined him, fired up the boat's engine, and

untied us. We were on our way. In keeping with

that morning's change in hunting routine, I

decided to also change things up a bit in my

fishing and find a different spot. As we glided past

our regular spot, Coop looked up at me as if to

say, "Aren't you going to stop? We're here," but I

kept on going.

Once we were about fifty yards past our normal spot, I snuggled up against the reeds, shut down the engine, and tossed out the anchor. We sat there in the boat, taking in the warm afternoon air and waiting for a fish to bite. The fish-finder was showing plenty of targets below the boat, so I figured it was just a matter of time.

Sure enough, a few minutes later, we had our first catch: a really nice bass. I was tempted to toss it in the live-well, but Cooper was just too excited to play with it, so I tossed it into the bottom of the boat. Cooper did his thing, picking it up and tossing it around. I was nervous that he would toss it overboard—it was such a nice fish—

but I figured we could always catch another one if he did.

As expected, the fish went over the side within a few minutes. But this time, Cooper followed. As he jumped off the boat, he tipped us so violently that I went head-over-heels into the water right after him. This wasn't the first time Cooper had tipped us, but it was the first time I went in, and I knew immediately that I was in trouble.

I was a good swimmer, but I was a sucker for putting on a bunch of gear whenever I went fishing or hunting, and all that extra weight was making it difficult for me to stay afloat. I struggled to keep my head above water. It felt like I was being pulled to the bottom by a huge rock

attached to my foot. I reached for the boat, which

was still anchored, but it had drifted out of reach

when we tipped over. The weight of my now-wet

gear was too much for me, and I went under.

I started to take off some of my clothes as I

drifted further below the surface, hoping that

would help. As I was taking off my lucky vest, I felt

a tug on the back of my collar. Slightly turning my

head, I saw that it was Cooper. He had my collar in

his mouth, and he was making a beeline for the

boat. I was in awe of his strength as he kept me

above the surface.

Once we reached the boat, I grabbed onto

the side, and Cooper released me. He swam

around to the back of the boat and used the stairs

I had built for him there. Soon, he was standing

over me. He reached down, grabbed the collar of

my jacket with his powerful jaws, and pulled me

up.

Safely back in the boat, I grabbed Cooper

and hugged him tightly, thanking him for saving

my life. He licked me on the cheek, and I loosened

my grip, grabbed him by the back of the ears, and

gave him a huge kiss on his nose. "Thank you,

buddy," I said, holding him tightly in a huge bear

hug. "I was in real trouble there."

I peeled off most of my wet clothes and

decided to fish a bit longer. I was a bit shaken, but

I my options were to either head home and

ruminate on my near-drowning or to continue fishing and try to put it out of my mind. Besides, Cooper wasn't done fishing, and I owned it to him to stay out there. We caught a few more fish, and then I called it a day.

Back at the cabin, I cleaned the fish we had caught and put them in the freezer on top of the many already frozen bags of fish. We were all set for many evenings of seafood dinners. I threw my clothes in the washer and took a hot shower to rinse off the lake water.

What a day: hunting, fishing, and nearly dying! Honestly, all I could do was smile about it. Coop and I had already had many adventures together, and I knew there would be more. This was the nature of country living, and I loved every minute of it.

Donning my robe, I walked out into the living room. I was a bit chilly, so I threw some logs in the fireplace and started a fire. The heat was soothing, and I sat on the carpet by the hearth, staring into the flickering flames. Cooper lay down next to me and put his head in my lap. I looked down at him, and tears welled up in my eyes. He had saved my life today, and there was no way I could ever repay him. "I love you, buddy," I whispered, scratching him behind the ears. His tail thumped against the floor a couple of times, and then he closed his eyes. He soon fell asleep.

As I sat there in front of the warm fire, I

thought about everything I had been through with

Sam and now with Cooper. For the first time in a

very long time, my hurt for the loss of Sam had

diminished and I felt content. I was still sad over

losing Sam, but I was so grateful that I now had

Cooper. Sam would have loved him, and she

would have loved living in this cabin. I smiled and

leaned back against our chair, closed my eyes, and

drifted off to sleep.

Chapter Eighteen

The years seemed to pass in the blink of an eye, and before I knew it, we were celebrating Cooper's eighth birthday. Steve came over for the celebration and teased Cooper about his new grey hair around his muzzle and over his eyes. I told him that he looked distinguished, but Steve insisted he was becoming an old man. In truth, even at eight years old, Cooper was still in great shape. He was muscular, very active, and showed no signs of slowing down.

We ate our traditional cupcakes, and after donning our "country" clothes, we headed out to take a walk around the lake. Steve and I brought shotguns in case we kicked up some birds along

the way. We took the same route that had ended

in a skunk encounter a few years earlier, and I

reminded Coop to not get too far ahead again.

"Otherwise, it'll end in a tomato-juice bath again,"

I joked.

At that, Coop sat down beside me and put

his ears back as if he understood me and was

begging me to take a different route. I smiled at

him, patted him on the head, and said, "Let's go,

Coop!" He jumped up, and we set off.

The memory of that skunk encounter also

brought back the memory of my even-longer-ago

bear encounter. I remind myself to be careful and

keep an eye on our surroundings. Many people

think you can't "accidently" come across a bear,

due to their size, but bears are really good at

hiding. Often, you don't have much notice before

you're in a dangerous situation.

As we walked along, Cooper lead the way,

his nose to the ground, searching for anything

that he could scare up for us to shoot. Steve and I

talked about my life at the cabin, and he told me

about his new job. He admitted that it was time to

stop living off of his parents and to start pulling his

own weight. He said that he had just started work

as a car salesman, and I laughed at the image.

"That's perfect for you, Steve," I chucked.

"Why do you say that?" he asked, crinkling

his brow.

"Well, you're a great talker and, more often than not, full of crap."

Steve squinted his eyes and shook his head. He knew I was right, but didn't want to admit it. Steve had only been on the job for a little over a week, and he had already sold seven cars. I think he had finally found his calling.

Suddenly, a pheasant jumped up, and Steve took aim and shot. The pheasant tumbled through the air and landed with a thump. Cooper was right there to pick it up and bring it back to me.

Steve looked mildly offended as Cooper trotted right past him and up to me. "What am I, chopped liver?" he quipped.

I handed the bird to him and explained,

"He's just used to bringing it to me. Don't be offended." I scratched Cooper behind the ear and praised him: "Good boy, Coop."

After receiving his praise for a job well done, Coop headed out front again to find another critter to flush out. Steve and I stayed back about ten feet to allow Coop to work his magic unencumbered.

"It sure is fun watching him work," Steve said.

"Yeah, it's my favorite part of hunting."

We continued to walk and chat, enjoying the falling leaves that made a rustling sound under our boots as we stepped. The air smelled of wet leaves.

HUGS

At times, Cooper would catch a scent and bury his head under the leaves, sniffing profusely. Steve and I would stop for a moment to see if Coop was on to something, but he would eventually raise his head, look around, and then continue on. I wasn't sure what he was smelling, but it was certainly odd behavior for him.

We had gone another fifty yards or so when my heart sank, and I realized what Cooper had discovered: the scent of a bear. No more than fifteen or twenty yards ahead, a momma bear lifted her head out of the tall grass to see what was approaching. Right beside her, two smaller heads appeared. A momma and her cubs, great. This was not what I had hoped to come upon.

All three of us stopped in our tracks and

froze like statues, our eyes locked on the bears.

The momma bear stared moving her head from

side to side, sniffing the air for clues about what

she was looking at. We all stood there for what

felt like forever, staring at one another as the bear

smelled the air. Steve and I held our breath,

unsure of what would happen next.

Then, a moment later, the momma bear

turned, leapt to the left, and disappeared into the

tall grass. It was silent for a few seconds, and then

the sounds of a fight erupted, confusing us. I

quickly saw that she was fighting off a huge

cougar. It had probably been stalking the bear

cubs and now found itself in an unexpected fight

to the death with the momma bear.

Seizing the opportunity to escape, Steve, Coop, and I started to slowly back away, retracing our steps along the path. Once we were far enough away to feel safe, we stopped to watch the battle. It was incredible to witness these two enormous animals grappling with and clawing at each other, both growling and biting to gain an advantage. The bear was slightly bigger and stronger, but the cougar was quick and agile.

As the pair fought, the bear cubs took off in the opposite direction. We couldn't see them through the tall grass, but we were able to follow their path by watching the grass move. The fight continued even after the cubs had escaped.

The bear landed a blow against the cougar's side, leaving a streak of blood-covered lines on its hide. The cougar leapt in the air and bit down on the bear's neck just behind the head and held on. The bear thrashed, trying to shake the cougar loose, but its jaws were too strong. We could see that the bear was getting tired and that the cougar now had the upper hand, but momma bear was determined to protect her cubs and wasn't ready to surrender.

As the battle raged on, I spotted movement from the corner of my eye. Coming out of the trees to the right was the biggest black bear I had ever seen. He was enormous and moving toward the fight like a freight train at full speed. He leapt right into the fray, and in an instant, the bears had the upper hand.

To my amazement, the papa bear—I assumed that's who he was, based on his size—grabbed the cougar by the nape of its neck and threw it several feet in the air. It was astounding to see him the huge cat tossed like a rag doll. The momma bear crouched down on all fours, trying to recover from the huge cat's assault. Now that papa bear had come to her rescue, she had a moment to rest.

The cougar landed, rolled on the ground, and snapped back up immediately to assess its new foe. The papa bear raised himself up on his back legs and roared. He must have been at least eight feet tall, and his huge paws were sported

claws so big, we could clearly see them from the

distance.

The cougar wasn't quite ready to give up

yet, though, and it sprang forward at the papa

bear. Anticipating the cougar's attack, the bear

swiped at it, tossing it aside with little effort.

Gathering itself, the cougar seemed to realize that

it was greatly overmatched. It growled again,

turned, and took off into the woods to the left.

The papa bear dropped to all fours and

quickly ran over to help the momma bear. He

stood over her for a few minutes as she gathered

herself and slowly began to walk with a slight limp

into the woods to our right. Papa bear followed

her, and soon they were out of sight.

Steve and I stared at each other in amazement. "That was wicked," Steve gushed.

"Yeah, holy crap," I replied, "I've never seen anything like that before."

Cooper seemed indifferent and looked around as if nothing had happened. I guess to him, that was just normal behavior.

Fearing that the cougar was still around, we turned and headed back to the cabin. I frequently looked back over my shoulder to make sure we weren't being stalked by either the cougar or the bears. I felt uneasy and vulnerable after watching that incredible encounter and realized that if put in that situation, I wouldn't last a minute. The sheer power of those animals was intimidating and impressive.

As we made our way home, Cooper flushed a good-sized brown rabbit out of some bushes. I took aim and shot, and the rabbit tumbled to the ground. As always, Cooper was Johnny-on-the-spot, picking up the rabbit and dropping it at my feet. I pocketed the rabbit, and we continued on.

Steve offhandedly mentioned that he loved rabbit, and I caught the hint and invited him to dinner.

Back at the cabin, Steve and I reflected on the day's events while we cleaned the pheasant and rabbit. Cooper lay on the floor of the shack, using the time to take a brief nap. Once done, we brought our dinner back to the cabin and dropped

the meat into some marinade. I started a fire, and

we took turns showering and changing into our

evening clothes. I put dinner in the oven, and we

all relaxed in the living room, taking in the heat of

the fire. Steve and I sipped our glasses of scotch,

neat, with no ice. Steve had brought over a bottle

of Pappy to help celebrate Cooper's birthday, and

he and I raised a glass to our incredible day in the

woods. Cooper jumped up into my lap and made

himself comfortable.

After a few glasses of scotch and much

reminiscing, we sat down to dinner. The pheasant

and rabbit were delicious, and of course, we both

shared some of our meals with Cooper.

166 | P a g e

After dinner, we cleaned up the kitchen and retired to the living room, where I put a couple more logs on the fire. It was dark outside now, and we could hear the hoot of owls nearby. "This place is so tranquil," Steve said, taking a draw of his scotch.

"Tranquil?" I said, looking over at him with a sarcastic smile on my face.

"Yeah, tranquil," he repeated. "Believe it or not, I do have a few big words in my arsenal."

I burst out laughing, and Cooper lifted his head off my chest to see what had made me laugh so hard.

We sat there for hours, just talking and sipping our scotch. We talked about Sam and the great times we'd had together. We talked about my suicide attempt and how much I had grown since then. I filled Steve in on all of my adventures with Cooper over the years.

Steve looked over at Cooper and I snuggled up in the chair together and said, "You know, Cooper is getting up there now. Any thoughts of getting him a little brother?"

I looked down at Coop and said, "No, not really. Cooper's got another eight years or so in him. He's in better shape than either of us."

Steve smiled and said, "Well, you should at least think about it. It'll take some time to train a puppy, and I'm sure Cooper would be more than happy to teach him everything he needs to know."

"Yeah, I'll think about it," I replied and took another sip of my scotch.

We decided to play a couple games of cribbage before calling it a night. By about two in the morning, the fire was nearly out, and we were exhausted. We got up and made our way to the bedrooms. "'Night, buddy," I said, patting Steve on the back.

"'Night, dude," he replied before disappearing behind the door to his room.

Coop and I hopped into bed, and I lay there for a while, reflecting on the day. I was truly lucky to have Steve and Cooper in my life. I was also very grateful that none of us had been eaten by a bear or cougar that day. As much as I loved the outdoors and wouldn't trade this life for anything,

I was also acutely aware of nature's power and

how fragile we were in the whole scheme of

things. In many ways, the danger makes it all that

much more enjoyable and exhilarating. I closed

my eyes and was soon fast asleep.

Chapter Nineteen

We all got up before the sun the next morning, having only slept about four hours. Still, we didn't seem to be tired. I brewed some hot coffee, and we sat at the kitchen table, sipping our wonderful morning nectar and watching Cooper gobble down his food. Then Steve rose from his chair and announced that he had to take off. Cooper and I walked him out and following a few hugs and pats on the back, Cooper and I watched him drive away and disappear around the bend.

"How about some fishing?" I asked Coop, who promptly sprinted off toward the dock. I went back into the cabin, put on my fishing clothes, filled my thermos with the rest of the coffee, and headed down to the dock. Cooper was already in the boat, patiently waiting for me. I fired up the engine and slowly pulled away from the shore. Cooper took his usual position in the bow of the boat, making sure that we were going in the proper direction and toward our favorite fishing spot.

Once there, I cut the engine and tossed out the anchor. Clouds had moved in during our ride out, and it began to rain lightly as I threw out the first line. The fishing was usually better when it rained because the fish saw the impact of the raindrops on the water, thought it was food, and jumped for it. Having the fish all excited for food always seemed to increase our chances for more

action, and today didn't disappoint. This was a

good thing, because Cooper tossed the first

couple of fish I caught overboard, so I had to make

a few extra casts to make up for the lost fish.

Even though it had happened hundreds of

times, Coop still always seemed surprised when

the fish flew out of his mouth and splashed into

the water. At least he had learned by now that

chasing after them was a lost cause. I think he

remembers having to save my life and didn't want

to repeat the experience. I was certainly grateful

that he had learned that lesson. I was not eager to

make another trip to the bottom of the lake. After

that experience, I had rigged a buoy to a length of

rope and clipped it to my belt whenever we went out fishing. It was better to be safe than dead.

As I was reeling in a fish to complete our take for the day, Coop and I looked up to see a couple of beautiful swans folding their wings and landing on the other side of the lake, just inside of the shoreline reeds. These were the first swans we had ever seen on the lake, and it was a gift to watch them fly in. Swans are huge birds, all perfectly white with a black swish on their faces that reminds me of the Nike logo. They're regal birds, and based on their haughty behavior, they seem to know it.

Cooper and I watched them for a while; I didn't want to fire up the boat's engine and scare them off. However, we were both soaked to the

bone from the rain, and eventually, I decided that

we needed to head back. As expected, once I

started the engine, the swans took flight. After

hovering just above the water for a spell, they

gained altitude and turned away over the trees. I

increased our speed, and we raced back to the

cabin.

As we approached the dock, I spotted a car

parked in the driveway that I didn't recognize.

Coop noticed it, too, and gave out a deep bark. I

slowed the boat, and it gently nudged the side of

the dock. Cooper wasted no time in jumping out

of the boat onto the dock and making a beeline

toward the strange car, while I tossed the rope

over the post to secure our arrival. I was close

enough now to see the outline of someone sitting

in the car. Cooper was standing beside the driver's

door, barking. The stranger must have been

intimidated by Cooper's presence, because he

stayed in the car and waited for me to come up

from the boat. I thought this was funny, so I took

my time gathering our catch and making my way

up to the car.

As I approached, I called Cooper over to me,

and the stranger finally felt safe enough to exit

the car. Once he stepped out, I recognized him: it

was my taxidermist, Dan from the Little Country

Store in a small nearby town. "Hey, Dan," I said,

releasing Cooper so he could make the man's

acquaintance.

Dan's eyes widened, and he stood perfectly still as Cooper approached. Coop sniffed Dan's pant leg a few times, and then his tail started wagging. Dan reached down to pet Cooper, and they were instantly buddies. "He's quite the big dog," Dan observed, closing the car door behind him.

"Yeah, he's a sight, but in reality, he's a total baby," I said, turning to walk to the game-cleaning shed. "So what brings you out here today?"

"I have your deer head all done and wanted to bring it out to you."

"Oh, that's right!" I said, coming to a stop.

"Thanks, Dan. It's been a few months, and I have to admit that I'd forgotten all about it."

"No problem," Dan said as he walked to the back of the car and opened the truck. I hurried on to the shed, dropped the fish on the table, and walked back over to join Dan. He reached into the truck and pulled out the deer head. He had done a tremendous job, and the deer looked fantastic.

"That ought to look great in your place," Dan said, smiling.

"You bet it will," I said. "Come on in for a beer."

"Don't mind if I do." Dan carried the deer into the cabin.

"Just set it down over there by the

fireplace," I directed as I reached into the fridge

for a couple of drinks.

We sat down at the kitchen table, cracked

open our beers, clanked them together with a

simultaneous, "Cheers," and both took a long

swig. Cooper was in the living room, sniffing every

inch of the deer head.

"I assume you're going to mount it over the

fireplace?" Dan asked, taking another long draw

of his beer.

"Yep. It'll look great there."

After a comfortable pause, Dan remarked,

"You know, I ran into Steve earlier today. He came

into the store for a tin of chew."

"Really?" I replied, surprised. "He started

chewing? Crap, I didn't know that. He spent the whole day here yesterday and never mentioned it."

"I think he doesn't want you to know but I thought I'd tell you so you can give him a hard time," Dan said.

"Rest assured, I will." I took another long draw on my beer, annoyed and frustrated with Steve. He had enough vices in his life, this is the last thing he needs to be doing.

Dan took a drink and then said, "Steve also mentioned that you might be looking for another puppy as Cooper starts to get up there in years."

"Yeah, we talked about it a little," I said, "but I'm not sure it's time yet. Cooper is doing great, and we really have a good thing going

here."

"Well, just so you know, we just started to

take in puppies to sell for Elaine down the road.

You know Elaine, right?"

"I've met her a couple of times at the store,

she's great lady. Is she breeding dogs now?" I

asked.

"She is, and guess what breed," Dan said

with a huge smile.

"Let me guess: chocolate labs," I replied,

feigning surprise.

"That's right, and they come from a

champion momma and papa. Come by the store

and check them out. You might get the itch to

take one home."

"I'll be by in a few days. I need some groceries, and I'm getting low on ammo," I said with a slight tone of dismissal.

"Great, I'll set aside your regular order of ammo. Is there anything else you want me to set aside... a lab puppy perhaps?" I gave Dan my best "nice try" face, and he laughed out loud. With that, he finished his beer and got up from his chair. "I have to be going. You two take care, and I'll see you in a few days."

I walked him out, and Dan hopped in this car and drove off. Then I made my way over to the shed to clean our fish from today. Once finished, I went back into the cabin for a hot shower. On the way into the bathroom, I peeked into the living

room and saw that Cooper was still sniffing the

deer head. I wondered what could possibly be so

interesting that he would have to spend so much

time investigating it, but he wasn't hurting

anything, so I headed off to take my shower.

Afterwards, I dressed and grabbed the

rather large hook and a hammer from the closet

by the front door. I wanted to hang that deer on

the wall and wasn't going to wait another minute.

I affixed the hook to the wall above the fireplace

and heaved the deer head up and onto the hook.

It fit snuggly to the wall.

I stepped back and admired my work. "That

looks great," I said. "What do you think, Coop?"

He put his paws on the fireplace and tried to stretch himself up to sniff it again, but it was now too high for him to reach. I shooed him aside and threw a few logs on the fire.

Once I had the logs burning, I went into the kitchen and grabbed another cold beer. I plopped down into our soft leather chair, set my beer on the side table, and motioned for Cooper to join me. He jumped up onto my lab and laid his head on my chest. I picked my beer up again, took a sip, and admired how nice the deer looked above the fireplace. The new addition seemed to make the cabin even more rustic than it already was, and a warm feeling of contentment washed over me.

I finished my beer and enjoyed the fire as

well as the sound of Cooper snoring on my chest.

It wasn't long before I closed my eyes and drifted

off to sleep. Another day was done, and it couldn't

have been any better.

Chapter Twenty

Another year passed in what seemed like a heartbeat.

One beautiful fall morning, I spent the early-morning hours chopping wood and doing some minor maintenance on the cabin. A few shingles on the roof had come loose, and the porch railing was wobbly in a few places, so I attended to them. After I was satisfied with their repaired state, I filled my coffee cup and sat down on the porch to take in the fresh air and listen to the birds sing. I caught sight of Cooper down by the lake, sniffing around.

After a few minutes, he picked up

HUGS

something from the grass, ran to the end of the

dock, and dropped it in the water. He did this a

couple more times, and my curiosity soon got the

better of me, so I walked down to the lake to see

what he was up to. As I got closer, Coop looked up

at me and wagged his tail. Then he went back to

work.

I was now close enough to see what Cooper

was doing. He was gently picking up frogs in his

mouth, walking them to the end of the dock, and

dropping them into the water. He was saving the

frogs! I watched in amazement as he picked up

one after another and walked them to the water.

He mouthed them so gently, I was certain that not

one was injured in the transfer. Good old Coop

was an incredible animal, with a heart as big as the moon.

He continued his rescue expedition until he couldn't find any more frogs, and then he proudly trotted up to the porch and lay down at the top of the steps, facing the lake so he could keep an eye on things. He didn't want to miss another frog in desperate need of help.

As I sat on the porch with Cooper and sipped my coffee, an unfamiliar car came down the driveway. Cooper jumped up and ran down the steps to investigate. The car came to a stop, and to my complete surprise, Sam's parents climbed out. Cooper jumped up on my father-in-law and gave him a huge welcoming lick across his face—just what Bill wanted, I'm sure. Coop then

walked around the car and introduced himself to

my mother-in-law, Judy.

I was shocked to see them. It had been nine

years since I had moved out to the cabin and

almost ten years since Sam's death. In all that

time, this was their first visit. Hellos and hugs

were exchanged as I welcomed them to the cabin.

I gave them the two-cent tour, and then we

settled down on the front porch to catch up. Bill

and I had a beer, and Judy enjoyed a hot cup of

coffee. I told them about all of my adventures

with Cooper, and they told me about their

retirement and travels overseas. We talked about

Sam and told heartfelt stories from our far-too-short time with her. It was really nice to see them.

After a couple of beers and a couple of hours, Bill

opened up about why, after all this time, they

decided to come and visit. "A few months ago, Bill

began, I was diagnosed with cancer". My heart

sank and I didn't know how to react. "I'm so sorry

to hear that, Bill", I said. Bill began again, "Well,

under the circumstances we felt that it was time

to make things right and let you know that we

don't think it was your fault for Sam's death. It

was an accident. You are family, and even though

we got off to a rough start, we always knew that

Sam loved you and we were happy that you were

in her life". I stood up with tears in my eyes and

hugged both Bill and Judy. "Thank you so much for

saying that Bill, I really appreciated it." We sat back down and chatted for a while longer about life and happiness. We all missed Sam so much and it was nice to talk about her again. Finally, they said their goodbyes and left. I told them to not be strangers, and they promised to visit more often.

As my in-laws disappeared down the driveway, I asked Cooper if he wanted to go for a walk. His ears perked up, and that tail of his started wagging a mile a minute. I went inside, put on my boots and cowboy hat, filled my thermos with the remaining coffee that Judy hadn't finished, and strapped on my pistol, just in case I wanted to do a little shooting practice.

I always loved the sound of the leaves

cracking under my boots as we walked, and this

day was no different. As always, Cooper was up

ahead, sniffing the trail and looking up from time

to time to see if whatever he was smelling was

still around.

We were barely fifty yards into our walk

when I spotted movement in a tree along the trail

no more than twenty yards out. Cooper walked

back to where I was and sat down next to me. He

had spotted the movement as well—probably

before I did, in fact—and his eyes were fixed on it.

The movement stopped, and after a moment or

two, the light breeze brushed away some leaves,

and I caught a glimpse of what had been causing

it: a cougar was perched on a low branch jutting

out over the trail. It was in the perfect spot to

launch an attack on an unsuspecting meal.

My first thought was worry over how close

this cat was to the cabin, and I started trying to

think of a way to scare it off. I wanted to make it

clear that this was my territory and that it needed

to find another place to do its hunting.

I inched a little closer to get a better look,

and Cooper took off down the trail toward the

cougar. I screamed for him to stop, but his ears

were back, and he was in a full sprint. I pulled out

my pistol and took off after him. As Cooper

approached the cougar, the huge cat jumped

down from the tree and landed right on top of

him. They locked together in battle and rolled on

the ground, looking like one big ball of fur going

head over heels. When they came to a stop, they

separated and stood face-to-face. They were both

in a crouched stance, baring their teeth and

growling at one another.

Even at roughly 125 pounds, Cooper was no

match for the huge cougar, and I knew I only had

a few seconds before it would be over. Before I

could react, Cooper shocked me by attacking. He

grabbed the cougar by the side of the neck and

held on for dear life. The cougar belted out a loud

growl and shook his body to get Cooper to release

his bite. It worked, and as soon as Cooper let go,

the cat took his turn and swatted at Coop, hitting

him on the side of the face. He tumbled to the ground and with a yelp.

The cougar was about to leap on Coop when I fired a shot into the air. Startled and confused, the cat turned to face me. I was only a few feet away, but I had that pistol aimed right at its head. I raised my pistol, fired another shot into the air, and quickly retrained my aim.

The cougar decided that it wasn't interested in fighting me. It turned, flashed a glance at Cooper, who was lying on the ground, and took off into the woods. As it ran off, I noticed some scars on his side, and I realized that this was the same cougar we had watched battle the papa bear the previous year. This cat was clearly a problem, and I decided right then what my next

hunting expedition would be.

I ran over to Cooper, who was now sitting

up, but still a bit wobbly. The left side of his

muzzle and his left ear were bleeding. He stood up

on all fours and shook his head, spraying blood all

over the front of my jacket. His tail was wagging

again, so I wasn't too worried about him in the

short term. "Let's go, Coop," I said, and we quickly

headed back to the cabin.

Once there, I lead Cooper to the truck and

headed straight to the vet. It was fairly late in the

afternoon and the clinic was about to close.

Cooper and I walked in, and the vet immediately

ran over to inspect him. He led us to the first

examination room on the right. It took the both of

us to get Cooper up on the examination table.

Once there, the vet began to examine his wounds

more closely. "What happened here?" he asked.

"Coop decided it was a good idea to pick a

fight with a cougar."

The vet looked up at me in surprise and

said, "You're lucky this is all that happened." He

went back to examining Coop, and after a few

minutes, added, "He's going to need some stiches

on his muzzle right here and on his ear right

here." He pointed the areas out so I could see.

"You can stay in the room if you want. Otherwise,

you're welcome to wait in the lobby while I fix up

old Coop."

"I'll stay right here with him, if that's okay," I replied, not moving an inch.

"No problem," the vet said. He gave Coop a few shots to numb the injured areas and then began to stich him up.

Cooper must have understood that the vet was helping him because he barely moved at all the whole time. Once he was finished, the doctor placed a couple of very sticky bandages on Coop's face and ear, and with that, we were ready to leave. Before we did though, the doctor wanted to give Cooper a once-over physical, just to make sure there were no additional wounds that he may have overlooked. Satisfied that there were no other injuries, we helped Cooper down off the examination table and walked out to the lobby to

pay. I took Steve's credit card out of my wallet and

put the $1800 bill on the card. I smiled as I signed

the receipt, knowing that very shortly, Cooper and

I would be visited by our old friend inquiring

about the huge charge on his card. Well, he gave

it to me for emergencies, so I'm sure he will

understand.

Cooper and I headed home, where I

plopped down into the leather chair, exhausted

and relieved. Cooper jumped up into my lap, and I

gave him a huge hug. He licked my face and put

his head down on my chest.

As I thought back over today's encounter

with the cougar, a feeling of dread overcame me. I

could have so easily lost Cooper. Something had

to be done about that cat, and that something

would begin tomorrow.

Chapter Twenty-One

Coop and I woke up before the sun. I

walked out onto the porch and looked out over

the cold, dark expanse before me. Small clouds

formed and drifted off every time I exhaled. It was

a cold morning, very cold. The sky was still filled

with bright, twinkling stars. The horizon was just

beginning to turn orange, and the birds were

already up and going about their day. Cooper

trotted past me and out into the lawn to take care

of his morning business, and I turned and went

back into the cabin to get dressed and start my

coffee.

I put on my hunting clothes and filled my

thermos with coffee. By the time I was ready to go, the sun was just cresting the horizon, and the morning frost was beginning to melt and drip from the scant leaves still clasping onto their branches. Beams of orange light streamed through the windows and cast long lines across the floor.

Today, I would be going out alone. I knew that Coop badly wanted to go, but I couldn't chance another encounter between him and the cat. Besides, he was still recovering from his injuries, and he needed the rest. This would be the very first time we didn't leave the cabin together, and it made my heart heavy, but I knew it was the right thing to do. I gathered up my remaining gear, complete with my rifle, pistol, and rather large hunting knife.

I kneeled down, told Cooper that I would be right back, and kissed him on the top of his nose. Coop's ears went flat on his head, which made it that much more painful to leave him at home. I closed the door behind me and tested the handle to ensure that it was locked, then remembered to lock the doggie-door as well. Cooper needed to stay put.

As I started to walk down the trail, I checked again to make sure my rifle and pistol were both loaded and ready to go. I had no way of knowing whether I would find the cougar today, but I needed to be ready. I hoped that I wouldn't come upon the bears in the area. That would

certainly complicate things, and I had no desire to

shoot a bear.

The fallen leaves crunched under my boots,

and the air was still cold enough to display my

breath.

I had been walking for about twenty

minutes when I came to the opening in the forest

where we had most frequently come into contact

with bears, but today, it was quiet and still. The

only sounds were the chirping of the birds and the

rustle of the wind playing with the tall reeds.

I decided to turn left and walk along the

opening's tree line. I felt too exposed walking

straight through it and felt like the trees provided

more cover and a possible escape should the

bears decide to show up.

As I was making my way around the edge of

the clearing, I heard a twig snap a few yards

ahead. I stopped and listened. I heard another

twig snap and was now sure something was there.

I slowly raised the rifle to my shoulder and aimed

in the direction of the sound.

Just as I got my rifle into place, papa bear

rose up out of the reeds and reared up on his hind

legs. He was enormous. The last thing I wanted to

do was shoot a bear, but if he decided to charge, I

would have no choice in the matter. My eyes were

laser-focused on the bear, and he roared and

sniffed the air. Then he dropped back down on all

fours and stared to charge at me.

I had the aim of the barrel fixed on his head and was prepared to fire. The bear was rapidly closing the gap between us, and I placed my finger on the trigger, ready to shoot.

At that moment, I felt a huge weight on my back and a searing pain in my shoulder. I fell to the ground under the impact of whatever had hit me from behind. The rifle fell out of my hands and landed a few feet in front of me, just out of my reach. Whatever had hit me was standing on top of me, and I couldn't move.

I—and it—only had a few seconds before the bear would be on top of us. I turned my head just enough to see what was holding me down and heard the low growl of the cougar. In the

corner of my eye, I could see its face, but it wasn't

looking at me; its gaze was trained on the quickly

approaching bear that was now only a few feet

away. The cougar looked down at me, and we

locked eyes for only a second.

Everything was happening so quickly and

violently that I was certain I was going to die. The

pain in my shoulder was agonizing, and the cat's

weight smashing me into the ground made it that

much more intense.

Through all the chaos, I caught a flash of

brown hair in the corner of my eye. For a

moment, I thought the bear was on the verge of

trampling us, but then I realized that brown fur I

saw was coming from the other direction. It flew

over us at lightning speed. The cougar jumped off

of me, and I was able to move just enough to see

what was happening.

It was Cooper! He was standing in fighting

position right in front of the bear, and the cougar

was behind him.

I heard a shout in the distance and turned

to see what it was. Steve raced across the clearing

toward us. I heard Cooper yelp and quickly turned

back to him just in time to see the bear on top of

him. I reached for my pistol, took aim, and shot

the bear just above his right shoulder. He winced

and tumbled back, falling to the ground.

Cooper then turned, leapt at the cougar,

and sank his teeth into the side of the cat's giant

head. The cougar shook Cooper off and jumped

on top of him. I carefully took aim, but Cooper and

the cougar were tussling, and I didn't want to miss

the cat and hit Coop by mistake. But then I heard

another yelp from Cooper, as the huge cat swiped

its razor sharp claws across his body, and I

couldn't bear to hold back. I fired at the cat,

hitting it directly in the side—right through the

scars left by papa bear. The cougar stumbled off

Cooper and began to charge at me. I fired off

three more shots at point-blank range, and the cat

fell to the ground a few feet in front of me.

I scrambled over to Cooper just as Steve

arrived, breathing hard from his run. He doubled

over to catch his breath while I crouched over

Coop. He looked up at me and then lay his head

back down on the ground. I kneeled next to him

and placed my hand on his head. His injuries were

severe, and he was bleeding badly.

Mustering all my strength, I picked him up.

He whimpered from the pain. I held him tightly to

my chest and began to make my way back to the

cabin as quickly as I could. I would run for a bit,

then walk, then run again, then walk. I looked

down at one point, and Cooper had tears in his

eyes. I knew he was in terrible pain.

When we finally arrived at the cabin, I

climbed up onto the porch and sat down in a

chair, cradling Cooper in my arms and holding him

tight. He licked my face, and I kissed him on his

nose.

Steve came up the steps a few minutes later

and saw the two of us in an embrace. "Is he going

to be okay?" Steve asked quietly.

I had my face pressed up against Cooper's,

and I shook my head no. I could tell that his

injuries were too severe, the only vet clinic in the

nearest town was closed, and the only alternative

was the emergency veterinary hospital in the next

town, which was over an hour away. He would

never make it.

I held him tightly and could feel his slowing

heartbeat against my chest. I whispered to him

that I loved him. A moment later, he closed his

eyes, and the beating stopped. My heart broke all over again, and I started to cry. My whole body shook, and I held Cooper as tightly as I could. Steve placed a hand on my shoulder and said he was so sorry. Tears were running down his face, too.

I sat in that chair holding Cooper for more than an hour. I couldn't believe he was gone. Steve sat next to us, his hand on my shoulder, as we looked out over the lake. The entire time, not a word was spoken.

Finally, I broke the silence. "We need to bury him. Will you help me?" I asked, looking over at Steve. There was a small elevated area to the right of the front lawn between the lake and the forest where the trail wraps around. This is where

I wanted Cooper to be buried.

"Of course," he said, getting up from his

chair.

I hugged Cooper one last time and kissed

him on the head. Then I picked myself up out of

the chair, still holding Cooper tightly, and made

my way down to the mound. Steve went around

to the back of the house and grabbed a couple of

shovels from the garage. I gently laid Cooper on

the soft grass, and Steve and I began to dig. I had

to stop numerous times to wipe the tears from my

eyes. Each time I did, Steve would do the same.

Once we had a proper opening in the

ground, I picked up Coop and gently laid him in his

final resting place. That's when I realized that I couldn't bear to cover him up. I sat down with my back to the grave and gazed out over the lake. Steve took this as a cue and completed the job himself.

When Cooper's grave was completely covered, Steve sat down beside me and put his arm around my neck. Our tears began to fall again. We sat on that mound, looking out over the water and watching the sun slowly drop below the horizon. I thought about all the wonderful adventures Coop and I had had together at the cabin, and I was grateful for every moment.

That night, I sat down in our leather chair alone and longed for Cooper's hug. My tears came again, and the sadness was overwhelming. I

covered myself with a blanket and finally found

sleep.

Chapter Twenty-Two

I woke up early, having slept in the chair all night. I folded up the blanket and went into the kitchen to start coffee. I couldn't get Cooper out of my mind, so I got dressed, filled my thermos, and stepped out onto the porch. The air was warmer than usual for this late in the fall, and I sat down in the chair where I'd last held Cooper. My eyes immediately turned toward where Cooper was buried.

It was still dark out, and all I could see was the black shadow of the turned-up dirt on top of the mount. The sun had not yet turned the horizon orange, so I sat there for a bit and sipped my coffee. I noticed that Steve's car was still in the

driveway. *He must have spent the night*, I thought.

Despite the darkness, the birds were

already up, chirping and singing their morning

songs. Most of the leaves had already fallen from

the trees, creating rows of grey wood skeletons

standing motionless against the black sky. It was

starting to get light when I went back into the

cabin to refill my thermos.

I had to take my mind off Cooper, so I

changed into my hunting clothes, grabbed my

shotgun from the gun case, and headed out the

door. I said hello to Cooper as I passed his resting

place and told him that I missed him dearly. I

knew my hunt today would be different without

Coop, but I always felt better after our morning hunt, so I regarded it as a form of therapy.

I had only traveled a short distance when a pheasant jumped up in front of me. I took aim and shot, sending the bird cartwheeling through the air before it landed with a thud. I walked over, picked up the dead bird, and placed it in my back jacket pouch. I loved hunting, but it was so much more enjoyable with my buddy Coop.

I continued on, but not much else was stirring this morning. I spotted a group of turkey off in the distance, and they stood there and looked at me with curiosity. I couple of the birds gave off a loud gobble that echoed through the bare motionless trees. As I breathed in the warm fresh air, I paused to watch an owl high in the trees. He spun his head around, scanning the ground for movement, and every once in a while, he gave off a soft, deep hoot.

When I had finished my hunt, I approached the cabin and saw Steve on the porch, drinking his coffee. I waved to him and made my way over to Cooper's mound. I laid my gun on the ground and sat down next to my buddy's final resting place. I talked to him for a bit as I looked out over the lake. I told him about the pheasant I had gotten this morning and about the turkeys and owl I had seen. I told him that I missed him and that I would be back to visit often. Then I grabbed my gun and walked back to the cabin.

As I was cleaning the pheasant I had shot, it occurred to me that Cooper needed a headstone. Once I was finished with the bird and had put tonight's dinner in the fridge in the cabin, I walked out onto the porch to say hello to Steve. "I see you decided to stick around," I said.

"Yeah, I figured it would be better to wake up with somebody around. I didn't want you to feel all lonely and stuff," he said.

"Thanks, buddy. I appreciate it." I sat down in the chair next to him and said, "Say, I was thinking about making a headstone for Cooper. Do you think you could stick around a bit and help me out?"

"No problem."

We got up and walked down to the lake.

"What did you have in mind?" Steve asked.

"I want to find a nice-sized rock and engrave something on it," I said, scanning the shoreline.

"Hey, here's one that might do the job," Steve said, pointing to a rock that was settled into the mud, "but it might be a bit too big."

I walked over to examine it. "No, that's perfect," I said as I reached down and tried to pry it from the mud. "Wow, that sucker is in there deep. Grab hold of it on that side and help me pull it loose."

"Are you kidding me?" Steve chuckled.

"We'll never get it out of the mud that way. I have

an idea." He turned and walked back up to the cabin and over to his car. He opened the trunk, pulled out a long rope, jumped in the car, and drove it over the lawn toward the lake. A few feet from the waterline, he turned around and backed up. "Now watch this," he said. He looped the rope around the rock and affixed the other end to the hitch on his car. Then Steve climbed back in the car, revved the engine, and slowly began to take the slack out of the rope. Once it was tight, he pressed down on the accelerator, and the rock slowly emerged from the mud. It made a sucking sound as the mud pealed back from around the edges.

Once it was loose, Steve pulled the stone a

few feet into the lawn before stopping. "Well,

how about that?" he quipped as he walked back

to the rock, smiling. He took the rope off the rock,

untied it from the hitch, threw it back in the trunk,

jumped in the car, and drove it back to the

driveway.

"Wait, what are we supposed to do with it

now?" I called after him. *Why don't we just drag it

over to the mound this way?* I wondered.

As Steve walked back to me, he said, "We

can roll it over to Cooper and then try to figure

out how to get it up on the mound once we see

what we're up against." He positioned himself

behind the rock and put his hands against the

side. When I didn't move to join him, he asked,

"Little help here?"

"Really? You think we can just 'roll' this thing all the way over there?" I asked as I got into position next to Steve.

"I do. Use your legs so you don't hurt your back," he said, and we began to push. To my surprise, the rock rolled over, and once we gained some momentum, it was relatively easy to move. In fact, once it started rolling, it just kept on going.

Steve and I stopped, looked at each other, and smiled as the rock rolled down the lawn right toward Cooper's mound. Once there, it rolled halfway up the side before losing momentum and rolling back onto the lawn, coming to rest just a couple of feet away.

"See? Piece of cake!" Steve declared,

walking over to the rock.

"Okay, but now what?" I asked with a

furrowed brow. "How are we going to get that

huge rock up the mound?"

"Inch by inch, my friend," Steve mumbled

while scrounging in the trees for a huge stick.

"What are you planning to do with that?" I

asked when he emerged with one he deemed

suitable.

"Leverage, oh you of little faith," Steve said.

"Now you push, and I'll use the stick to wrench it

up there."

"This outta be interesting," I muttered, but I

began to push.

Steve placed the stick at the base of the rock and pushed up on the other end. I was astonished that it was actually working. Working together, we moved that huge rock up the mound little-by-little until we reached the top. We gave it one last push, and it was perfectly positioned next to Cooper.

"And *that*, my friend, is how we do it." Steve tossed the stick back into the trees.

I shook my head and smiled at him. "Alright, let me get my tools," I said and walked back to my workshop to get what I needed.

Steve went into the cabin and met me back at the mound with a couple cups of hot coffee. "Break time," he said, handing me a cup and sitting down next to the rock.

I sat down next to him, and we sipped our coffee and gazed out over the water in silence together. I heard the owl hoot again and commented that it was odd that he was still out, considering they were nocturnal.

Steve joked that he was probably watching us and laughing his tail feathers off. I looked at Steve and smiled.

Once we finished our coffee and were well-rested, I grabbed my tools and began working on the rock.

"I'm going back to the cabin to destroy your plumbing," Steve declared, and off he went.

Again, I shook my head and got to work. I

was careful to take my time, and after about an hour or so, the work was done. Steve came back just as I was finishing, and he supervised the last few minutes.

"Looks good," he said and then read it aloud: "'Here rests my buddy, Cooper. He gave the best hugs.' Well said." Steve clapped me on the back and added, "Now let's get back to the cabin. I have a surprise for you."

"I already have a blow-up doll," I joked.

"It's not that, dummy. Just follow me."

I picked up my tools and followed Steve to the cabin. Having had plenty of experience with Steve's "surprises," I was simultaneously excited and afraid.

Chapter Twenty-Three

As I walked through the door, Steve was

already standing there, facing me and grinning

from ear-to-ear.

"What?" I asked nervously.

"Notice anything different?" He held out his

arms as if gesturing to the entire place.

"No, what did you do?" I asked, looking

around.

"Keep looking."

And then I saw it. A tiny brown head peeked

around the back of my favorite leather chair. He

tilted his head, and his ears went up. His striking

blue eyes met mine, and he put his paws up on

the armrest of the chair. His tail started to wag

excitedly.

"Surprise!" Steve yelled.

I walked over to the chair and picked the

puppy up. A red ribbon was loosely tied around

his neck, covering up his brand-new collar. I held

him in my arms, and my eyes welled up. "You got

me another chocolate lab," I choked out. I was

struggling to speak through the lump in my throat.

"Yup, and he comes from the same mom

and dad as Cooper," Steve proudly stated.

"Holy smokes! They must be like twelve

years old."

"Yeah, I had to slip the old guy some Viagra

to get the job done," Steve quipped.

I laughed and then paused, considering.

"No, you didn't... did you?" I honestly wasn't sure
if he was kidding or not.

"Of course not, you idiot," Steve replied.
"He pooped on the floor in the hallway, but I
cleaned it up, so no worries. I guess he's not potty
trained yet."

"Wait, when did you get him?" I asked,
confused. The timing didn't add up.

"Well, that's something I wanted to talk to
you about," Steve said. He sat down at the kitchen
table. I sat down as well, still holding the new
puppy who insisted on licking my face and biting
my ear. "I actually picked him up yesterday on my
way out here to visit you guys. Cooper was getting

a bit older, and I thought it would be cool to have

a puppy around for him to mentor. But when I got

here, you were nowhere to be found, and Cooper

was in the cabin. Something didn't feel right.

Then, when I opened the front door to see if you

were out on the porch, Coop ran right past me

and darted into the woods. I'm so sorry, dude. I

didn't know what was going on, and I didn't mean

to let him out. He was so quick, I didn't have time

to stop him. But if I hadn't let him out, he would

probably still be alive. I'm so, so sorry." He

lowered his head, and tears dripped onto the

table.

"Steve, it wasn't your fault. You didn't know

what was going on," I said, reaching out and

putting my hand on his shoulder. When he didn't respond, I asked, "You said you got the puppy yesterday?"

Steve lifted his head. "Yeah, I wanted to surprise you and Coop."

"How did you keep him quiet for the last twenty-four hours?"

"Duct tape," Steve said, smiling.

"Oh no, you didn't," I said in a scolding tone.

"Of course not," he replied. "I kept him in the work shed overnight and slept by him on the floor. I closed the extra bedroom door so you'd think I was sleeping in there."

"Nicely done, my friend," I said, patting him

on the shoulder.

"Well, what are you going to name him?" Steve asked.

"Trigger," I replied. I didn't even have to think about it. "I've always liked that name and he will be a hunter, just like Coop."

"Trigger it is," Steve said and got up from his chair. "Listen, I have to take off, but I'll be back in a couple of days to see how you two are getting along."

"I don't know what to say, Steve. Thank you so much."

He gave me a quick hug and a slap on the back. "My pleasure."

Trigger and I walked Steve out and watched

him drive out of sight. Then I put Trigger down,

and we walked over to the mound so I could

introduce him to Cooper—his big brother.

We made our way to the top of the mound,

and Trig was sniffing everything in his path. I sat

down next to Cooper's rock and watched Trigger

work his way around the mound, taking in every

new scent he could find. He stopped at Cooper's

grave and sniffed it for a very long time. Then he

looked up at me and tilted his head, as if he knew

what was in there. I called him over, and he

jumped into my lap and snuggled up against me,

putting his head against my neck. My hugs were

back.

I placed my hand on Cooper's rock, smiled,

and looked out over the water. I thought about all the adventures Trig and I would have together. Cooper had saved my life in so many ways, and I would miss him dearly.

As we sat there, taking in the beautiful scenery, there was a rustle in the bushes nearby. Trig heard it and immediately jumped out of my lap to go investigate. Rooting around in the bushes, he froze in a perfect point, his tail straight in the air. I got up and walked over to see what he had discovered. I approached slowly, and as I approached the bushes, a nice big pheasant jumped up, cackling, and flew off to the other side of the lake.

I looked down at Trigger and said, "Let's go

get our hunting gear and get that bird."

Trigger started wagging his tail and turning

in circles. And so it started all over again, and I

couldn't be happier.

NOTES

NOTES

Other Books by Pete Klein

Christmas Morning

https://www.amazon.com/gp/product/B075DH6L4C/ref=dbs_a

_def_rwt_bibl_vppi_i7

First Date

https://www.amazon.com/gp/product/B075W2MYVH/ref=dbs_

a_def_rwt_bibl_vppi_i4

Walk to the River

https://www.amazon.com/gp/product/B07582JTJP/ref=dbs_a

def_rwt_bibl_vppi_i6

Unwavering Choices

https://www.amazon.com/gp/product/B07MZLY31J/ref=dbs_a

def_rwt_bibl_vppi_i0

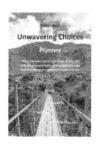

Unwavering Choices – Planner

https://www.amazon.com/gp/product/1795240326/ref=dbs_a

def_rwt_bibl_vppi_i2

Unwavering Choices – Book Journal

https://www.amazon.com/gp/product/179524299X/ref=dbs_a

def_rwt_bibl_vppi_i3

Unwavering Choices – Author Cookbook

https://www.amazon.com/gp/product/1795763043/ref=dbs_a

def_rwt_bibl_vppi_i1

Made in the USA
Monee, IL
22 December 2024

75067059R00142